A RENEGADE PASSION

"You win, Samantha."

Samantha stopped short as a figure stepped out of the shadows to tower over her. He walked close. She drank in the height and breadth of Matt, the thick dark hair underneath his weathered Stetson, the light eyes that were presently earnest, the strong features and generous mouth that raised such wild longings inside her. Her heartbeat escalated to thunder as he whispered his next words.

"I told myself that I came to see you tonight so we could talk. That sounded reasonable. But, everything changed as soon as I saw you. I want you now more than I have any right. You're all I've thought about since I first met you."

ELAINE BARBIERI

Renegade

LEISURE BOOKS NEW YORK CITY

A LEISURE BOOK®

July 2010

Published by

Dorchester Publishing Co., Inc.
200 Madison Avenue
New York, NY 10016

Copyright © 2010 by Elaine Barbieri

ISBN 10: 0-8439-6365-4
ISBN 13: 978-0-8439-6365-6
E-ISBN: 978-1-4285-0891-0

The name "Leisure Books" and the stylized "L" with design are trademarks of Dorchester Publishing Co., Inc.

Printed in the United States of America.

10 9 8 7 6 5 4 3 2 1

Visit us online at www.dorchesterpub.com.

Renegade

Prologue

His naked flesh brushed hers and he stifled a groan. He moved instinctively and his passion echoed inside her, sending her senses reeling. She accommodated his mouth and his kiss sank deeper. His tongue caressed hers. Her heartbeat thundered as he tasted and explored the aching flesh she offered him with a hunger she could not deny.

The heat intensified. The sweat of their mutual fervor bound them. She gasped when he suckled her breasts with gentle ferocity. Her need became a mindless hunger that matched his, and she wrapped her fingers in his hair to clutch him tight against her.

The torment accelerated.

The ecstasy heightened.

Their gasps were simultaneous when he entered her at last.

She wrapped her legs around him, drawing him closer, raising herself so he might sink more deeply inside her, exhilarating in the moment with a frenzy that she did not recognize as her own.

Colors flashed before her closed eyelids as their lovemaking became red-hot heat.

She held her breath as climax neared—but he paused. He looked down at her, his gaze passionate yet suddenly uncertain.

Why was he waiting? She loved him. Hadn't she proved that to him? He was everything she had ever wanted, everything she had ever needed.

Or—was he?

Then came the ultimate question. Was this the solution she had been seeking?

Chapter One

New York City, 1866

Samantha Rigg smarted inwardly as she closed the office door of the Pinkerton Detective Agency behind her and started toward the staircase. She was determined not to show her resentment as she descended rapidly toward the street with a stiff smile.

She had entered Allan Pinkerton's office only a half hour earlier. It appeared he had just moved into the office, so stripped was it of any personality with its barren walls and functional furniture, and with the large piles of files lying on his desk. She had learned quickly, however, that the space reflected the fact that she had entered a branch office of "The Eye That Never Sleeps," as well as the personality of a man dedicated to his work. Unfortunately, she had also learned that although intelligent, that same man was stubbornly dedicated to outdated Scottish notions.

Samantha stepped down into the lobby of the building, thinking that Allan Pinkerton had seemed happy to see her at first. He had smiled, his face alight at the sight of her. The Rigg name was the password. Her father, Thomas Rigg, had been one of his most successful operatives.

"Welcome to the Pinkerton Agency."

Unfortunately, those were the last truly pleasant words that Allan Pinkerton had spoken to her.

Samantha's lips tightened as she walked toward the street door, her heels clicking noisily. Her widowed father had been driven to the Pinkerton Agency because of his abhorrence for the lawlessness that seemed to be overtaking the country. She had adored him, and the feeling was mutual. He had refused to allow her slender stature, her delicate appearance, or her sex to influence her ambition while growing up. Her ability to outride, outshoot, and fight better than most boys her age had pleased him. He had seemed especially gratified when she was able to outsmart most of them, too.

Samantha's step faltered as she recalled being notified of her father's premature death from an outlaw's bullet when she was fourteen. That day was the worst in her life because she had known she would never see her dear father again. It was the best because her vocation was born.

Unable to withhold a frown, Samantha pushed open the door of the building and stepped out onto the busy New York sidewalk. The hectic city with its tall stone buildings and paved streets was unfamiliar to her, a young woman from a small upstate town.

Yet she ignored the crowded walk, as well as the carriages, wagons, and pedestrians all appearing to have an urgent destination in mind. She automatically joined the intense throng, her mind on the unintended harshness of Allan Pinkerton's response to her request.

She had traveled a long way to hear it. She had silently vowed never to forget it:

"The Pinkerton Detective Agency does not hire women who have no background in detective work, or women whose goal is to avenge their fathers' deaths—no matter how sincere they are."

That last addendum was meant to soften the blow of a refusal to employ her, but it did not. She realized now that she needed to prove to Allan Pinkerton that inheriting her father's ability to outsmart the average male, as well as the many hours she had listened intently while he explained every investigative detail of his many successes, was her unofficial training. Her own inborn tenacity provided the rest.

She also needed to show him that her desire was not to *avenge* her father, but to *honor* him.

She knew only one way to do that.

The bobbing of Samantha's blonde curls belied her strength of purpose as she started down the street in the direction of her lodgings. She was sure she could accomplish what other Pinkerton operatives could not because she had an advantage that Allan Pinkerton had considered a drawback.

That advantage was simple.
She was a woman.

Winston, Texas

Samantha leaned back against the bar of the Trail's End Saloon, her present place of employment. Winston was more humid than she had expected, and her purple satin dress did not suit the temperature. She attempted to pull the fabric away from her moist skin to afford herself more comfort. In doing so, she inadvertently lowered an already generous neckline even farther.

The male contingent at the bar stirred.

Samantha smiled at the realization of those fellows' thoughts. She would allow none of them to succeed in what they were thinking, of course, despite her knowing grin. She had used the tool of playing one male against another since childhood. She intended to use it wisely.

But she was still hot and uncomfortable.

She had learned from Sean McGill, a close Pinkerton friend of her father's, that a bank-robbing spree in Texas had decimated the profit of the Landover Syndicate, a well-known eastern consortium that had invested heavily in Texas. When the law failed to gain the proof needed to bring the thieves to justice, the Landover Syndicate hired the Pinkerton Agency to do it. Unfortunately, Pinkerton had failed also.

With Allan Pinkerton's response to her employment in mind, Samantha had made the decision to use part of the money she had inherited to travel to Texas, where she intended to show Pinkerton that *she* could get the proof he needed.

It had not taken her long, however, to reach the conclusion that Winston, Texas, was uncivilized in comparison with bustling New York City. It was even a step back in time from the diminutive upper New York State town of Bristol, where she was born. To her mind, it was the last place a successful bank robber would choose to make his base. Yet in the time since, she had done her homework, and she now understood the reason.

She had doubted her decision to come to Winston for the first time a month earlier when after a dusty, bumpy, hot journey, she had stepped down from a dilapidated stagecoach to find the town boasted a total of two unpaved streets—and nothing much else. Even Main Street was littered with potholes that she had learned the hard way would fill with ankle-deep mud after every rainstorm.

The first establishment that had met her disapproving eye had been the Trail's End Saloon, which she had discovered was the town's only source of entertainment. The structure had been difficult to miss since the gaudily painted, false-fronted building alone had any traffic in the heat of midday. A single mercantile where ranchers bought their supplies sprawled nearby, and a livery stable that housed and offered horses for hire was located a distance away. The old fellow named Toby Larsen who owned the business had become an instant friend.

A stagecoach office—where a coach arrived weekly, if it arrived at all—was sandwiched between a small bank that served the entire community and an apothecary where a pharmacist of questionable ability presided. The doctor's office next door had been unoccupied since the demise of the town physician two years previously.

She had met the muscular fellow named Horace Trimm who owned a blacksmith shop where he sweated on a daily basis and watered nightly at the Trail's End. She had found him to be an honorable man. She had thought to patronize the small "French boutique" in the vicinity until she met the owner, a woman with a dubious accent and a decidedly haughty manner. A nondenominational church where a part-time preacher expounded on the penalties of sin each Sunday was situated at the far end of the street.

"Howdy, Samantha. How about letting me buy you a drink?"

Samantha's spontaneous smile flashed at the young fellow at her elbow. She had become the newest female attraction at the Trail's End Saloon. Her quick mind and saucy quips—plus more obvious female assets—had made her an instant success. It was her job to *entertain* the customers. The extent of that *entertainment* was at her discretion.

"Howdy, Jim. You're a bit early today, aren't you?" Her smile widened.

"Yes, ma'am, but I've been waiting to come here to see you since the sun came up this morning. I guess you're just about all I think about these days."

Samantha remained cynical of that remark as she studied him more closely. Jim Sutton was average in height and weight and had average coloring, but he was a sincere, hardworking fellow without a deceitful bone in his body. She intended to be at that establishment only a short time and she didn't want to lead him on.

She responded with a broadening of her smile. "I'm glad to hear that you consider me a friend, Jim, because I enjoy your company. But between you and me, I figure you ought to direct your attention more favorably toward Helen over there." Motioning toward the slender, young brunette who was obviously new to the game, she winked. "Helen's been talking about you a lot lately. Something tells me she sees something special in you that it would pay to cultivate."

Helen took that moment to glance their way, as if confirming Samantha's whispered confidence, and Jim raised his brow.

Samantha gave Jim a light shove. "I'm not here officially for a while yet, but Helen is, so make the best of it."

"But I came here to see you, Samantha."

"Maybe so, but like I said, I'm not here yet. So skedaddle!"

Appearing uncertain, Jim responded, "All right, if you'll promise to save some time for me later."

"That's a promise."

Samantha looked back at the street as Jim walked away, preoccupied with her thoughts. Since the Trail's End was the rumor mill of town, she had known it would be the best place to get situated. It didn't hurt any that it was also the most likely place for her to come into contact with the man she sought to bring to justice.

His name was Matt Strait.

A familiar tremor moved down Samantha's spine at the thought of him. There was something about the man that set her pulses racing. She mused unconsciously that perhaps it was the way he walked with unconscious male confidence. Or perhaps it was the intensity behind his all too brief smiles, or the hidden but potent quality in his gaze when he looked at her. She didn't like the fact that his light eyes seemed to burn wherever they touched her. Nor did she appreciate the feeling that—filled with amusement one moment and fierce the next—his gaze seemed to speak directly to her without an utterance of her name. The effect left her mouth dry.

Forcing herself to ignore her personal reaction to him, she had confirmed that Matt had been born and raised on a vast but practically bankrupt ranch just outside town left to him by his father. To hear the locals tell it, Matt was a hard worker who barely scraped by in his effort to save the ranch. It did not take her long to also learn that the ranch was the reason Jenny Morgan, his fiancée and a neighboring rancher's daughter, had not yet married.

Matt Strait had been an unpredictable, motherless boy with a wild streak, according to the townsfolk. They were now convinced he had changed as he matured, but she knew he had not changed at all. Matt Strait had simply chosen to lead a double life and support his failing ranch with the proceeds from his robberies.

Yet an inability to find proof of his actions had kept the law and Pinkertons at bay. Matt Strait had outwitted the best of them, but she was determined he would not outwit her.

Samantha's attention grew suddenly acute as the saloon's swinging doors opened.

Speak of the devil.

Samantha's heart began a gradual pounding as Matt Strait approached the bar with a few nods of acknowledgment at familiar greetings. The strange heat inside her stirred and she was intensely aware that her trembling when his gaze briefly caught and held hers had no relation to fear.

Samantha's breathing quickened. Yet she somehow resented the blatant, natural masculinity that had worked its way into her consciousness. She disliked her appreciation of the broad stretch of her quarry's shoulders, his narrow waist and male hips.

She found the gun belt casually strapped there as objectionable as her thought that he could handle any opposition without a problem. It annoyed her even more that the bulge just below his belt fascinated her.

She concluded with forced objectivity that Matt Strait's appeal was his appearance of being hardworking but slightly untamed. She was forced to concede, however, that in him she faced a danger she had not considered.

Watching him openly, Samantha knew that in a few minutes Matt would take his drink to a table in the corner to wait for an opening at the poker table. He made no pretense of being interested in her or in any of the other women at the Trail's End despite any advances made. He gave every appearance of being completely loyal to his fiancée.

Balderdash! She was certain there had to be a chink in his armor—and only a woman with her unofficial training could find it.

"That ain't the way to get your man, Samantha."

Samantha jumped at the voice beside her. She realized for the first time that Toby, the thin, bow-legged, gray-haired old man with the kind eyes who was the owner of the livery stable, stood beside her.

She responded with a wink. "Am I that obvious, Toby?"

"I'd say you are." The old fellow's gaze narrowed as he assessed her expression. "If you don't want to be no more obvious than you are, I'd say you shouldn't look at that fella that way."

"At Matt Strait, you mean?"

"Who else? I figure he's the reason you haven't given any of your admirers here a tumble."

"What do you mean, Toby? I'm nice to everybody."

"Yeah . . . nice, when fellas like Jim Sutton, Randy Jacobs, Lefty Morse, and a few others who aren't worth mentioning would like a little more than that."

"Toby," Samantha said jokingly, "you didn't mention yourself in that lot."

"Well, Samantha, it's like this." Toby's smile quirked. "If I was a few years younger and a heap prettier, I figure I might stand a chance. But the fact is, I know my limitations. You ain't looking for an old fella whose best days are behind him. All I got left in me now is real affection for you and some good advice, which I can offer freely."

Samantha replied, "So what is that advice, Toby?"

"Forget Matt Strait if you know what's good for you." Toby was suddenly sober. "I know the kind of man he is. He's sincere, and any interest you might stir up in him won't be for the long run. He's engaged to a real fine woman who will make him a good wife when his ranch is solvent. She's as plain as a church mouse and you ain't, but you can't compete with her when it comes to what she can offer a fella like Matt."

"I don't think I like what you just said, Toby. It sounded like you were saying I wouldn't make some man a good wife someday."

"Maybe you would, and maybe you wouldn't. I don't know. I just figure you're perfect the way you are." Taking a step closer, Toby said more softly, "But I've been watching you and I figure you ain't as world-wise as you make out to be. I figure you're heading for trouble and I'm just trying to get you to sidestep it, that's all."

"By staying away from Matt Strait."

"That's right."

"What if I don't want to stay away from him?"

"I'd say I think that fella's made it obvious that he don't come here to bother with women—you included. If you push him, you might end up sorry."

"Would you write me off then, Toby?"

"Samantha, honey," Toby said sincerely, "it ain't in my nature to do that. I'd stick by you to the end, whatever you decide."

"Well, in that case—"

Excusing herself, Samantha headed directly toward the table where Matt had sat. Her heartbeat accelerated. She was tired of wasting time. She needed to get close enough to Matt Strait so he'd talk freely to her, which was easier said than done.

Samantha continued her sultry advance. She sensed Matt wouldn't be able to resist her much longer, especially when she had done everything short of jumping onto his lap to wear down his reserve.

It occurred to her abruptly that perhaps it was time to do just that.

Comfortable at a table in the corner of the room, drink in hand, Matt kept his eye on the poker table. He knew that Jake Watson would quit the game soon. Like him, Jake spent only a few hours playing poker whenever he came to the Trail's End. He would leave soon. Matt would then take Jake's place before it grew dark—relaxation that he had thoroughly earned.

His breathing suddenly accelerating, Matt felt Samantha Rigg's advance toward him. He glanced at her and silently cursed. He remembered the first time he had seen her. She had been standing near the bar when he entered the Trail's End. It had been like being hit in the stomach, so breathless had the sight left him. Her hair had seemed to glow with a golden warmth of its own. Her creamy skin was tight over delicate cheekbones, and her eyes—he had never seen hazel eyes with sparks of gold that seemed to dance for him alone. She had shown an instant interest and had batted her heavily kohled eyelashes at him. Yet despite all her efforts since then, he had remained true to Jenny and had refused to change his comfortable routine.

Admittedly, however, coming to the Trail's End wasn't as relaxing as it once had been.

Matt looked away with renewed determination as Samantha continued walking toward him.

Jim Sutton watched Samantha's steady advance toward Matt Strait's table. He commented to the brunette sitting beside him, "It's easy to see the reason Samantha sent me over here. But by the look on Matt's face, I figure her thinking don't suit him too much, neither."

Helen frowned. So Samantha had sent Jim. She had wondered why he had left Samantha for her.

Helen unconsciously shrugged. It didn't matter why Jim had sought her out. She liked being with him. As a matter of fact, she liked Jim—more than liked him.

"I figure Samantha's in for trouble with Matt." Jim did not look away from Samantha. "She wouldn't be in for trouble with me."

"Maybe that's why she likes Matt." Jim turned toward her, and Helen hastened to add, "Samantha don't like things too easy."

Jim said simply, "I'm worried about her."

"No need to worry about Samantha. She's real nice, but she knows what she's doing."

Jim turned toward her with a frown, and Helen smiled. "Truth is truth, Jim."

Jim appeared to consider that response and finally sighed. "You're right. Truth is truth, but that don't make me like it any better."

Helen didn't like the way things were going, either.

Standing beside Matt moments later, Samantha waited until he finally squinted up at her. When he did, his heated gaze all but stopped her in her tracks. Yet she forced a coy tone and asked deliberately, "Did you come here to see me, Matt, honey?"

Matt's breathing quickened, betraying her effect on him. His intense perusal touched her almost palpably before he replied, "I came here to play cards, like I always do."

Warning bells sounded in Samantha's mind, but she responded as if unfazed, "Well, I guess I can change that if I try real hard."

Determined, Samantha sat on Matt's lap before he could reply and slid her arm around his shoulders. The bulge underneath her rounded backside was revealing, and she wiggled effectively.

Matt's expression was suddenly tight. "All right. I think it's about time you tell me what you want from me."

"I'd say it's obvious to everybody but you what I want."

"Really? You find me irresistible, is that it?" Matt's light-eyed gaze singed her. "I find that hard to believe."

"Are you trying to tell me no woman ever found you irresistible before?"

Matt's voice dropped a warning note softer. "You're playing with fire, Samantha."

"Am I?" Her lips hovered near his. "Well, maybe I like playing with fire."

Matt stared at her a moment longer. He then rasped, "Hell, I'm tired of fighting this."

Lifting Samantha to her feet, Matt stood up abruptly. He then pulled her along behind him as he headed for the door.

Uncertain what he intended when they emerged briefly out onto the street, Samantha gasped when Matt pulled her into a nearby alleyway and crushed her against the side of the building with his body. She did not expect his passion when he plundered her mouth with his and moved against her with unrestrained heat. Nor did she anticipate her involuntary response.

Somehow unable to help herself, Samantha joined his fervor. Trading him kiss for kiss and caress for caress, she struggled to run her hands against the muscles of his back, wanting more. She strained at the tightly belted waistband of his trousers as he caressed her tingling flesh.

The heat between them grew hotter.

Samantha was past rational thought when Matt drew her away from the wall and slid his arms around her. She was unaware of the exact moment when the plundering gentled and the loving began, but felt only the warmth of Matt's body as he clutched her tight against him. She groaned when his hands splayed wide against her back in ever-increasing hunger.

He clutched her closer still. He explored the intimate curves of her body. They were moving in mutual heat, writhing in mindless passion. They were—

Abruptly jerking himself back from her, Matt whispered hoarsely, "Don't sell yourself short, Samantha. You're real good. You can do better than cheap lovemaking in a dark alleyway, which is all you'll ever get from me."

Releasing her just as abruptly, Matt strode away.

Samantha stood stock-still. Her heavy breathing the only sound that broke the silence, she swallowed tightly and watched as he stepped out of sight on the street.

Leaving Samantha behind him, Matt strode toward the rail where his horse was tethered. He mounted, angry with himself for having given in to the beauteous tease. He nudged his mount into a gallop and headed out of town. Admittedly, he had almost fallen into the trap that Samantha had set for him, but he was now more determined than ever to ignore the attraction that had sprung up between them.

It was not difficult to understand why he was attracted to her. Samantha was the realization of any man's dream. The trouble was that he knew her type. His mother had been of her ilk—a beautiful dance hall woman who had surrendered to desire but who deserted his father as soon as she was able. She had not wanted to marry the decent man who loved her. Nor had she given a thought to him or to their son when she ran off and left his father to raise him.

Confused, Matt knew only that an emotion he could not name tightened deep inside him when he thought of Samantha Rigg. He also admitted to himself that a minute more in that alleyway, and he would have abandoned common sense.

Relieved that he could think clearly again, Matt slowed his horse to a canter on the trail back to his ranch. He reconfirmed in his mind that Jenny was the only woman for him. She didn't have hair the color of corn silk or eyes that both teased and hungered, but he had known her most of his life. He knew she was loyal and loving, and without a dishonest bone in her body.

Jenny was everything that Samantha was not.

Two words summed up the situation with Samantha.

Forget her.

Aware that she had lost control and that her quarry had not, Samantha took a shuddering breath as Matt mounted his horse and left town. She then raised her chin, adjusted her smeared makeup as best she could, rearranged her upswept hair, and smoothed her dress. Taking a breath, she strode cockily back through the swinging doors of the Trail's End. She knew what the men were thinking, and she knew what she needed to do.

Samantha walked boldly toward the piano and muttered a few words to the old fellow seated there. She waited for her music to begin and then sang a loud, audacious tune until those same fellows laughed out loud. Thunderous applause accompanied the last line of the song, and Samantha smiled broadly.

But the truth was, she wasn't laughing.

Chapter Two

A bright midday sun shone on the street beyond as Samantha stood again at the Trail's End bar. The stench of perspiring bodies grew stronger in the afternoon heat, but she still preferred it to the pervading smell of stale beer and red-eye. In order to do her job, she also tolerated the heavy smoke that hung overhead despite the early hour; the shrieks of feminine laughter from either Lola, Maggie, Denise, or Paulette—Helen was not an offender—and the endless noise generated by the slap of cards and responsive moans of dispirited men at the busy gaming tables. A gentle but untalented fellow named Otto banged out continuous and unrecognizable tunes at the ancient piano, adding to the din.

Despite the early hour, several of her most persistent and ardent admirers had gathered—cowboys who truly believed a lucky one of them would have his attention rewarded with some private time with her. None appeared to realize that she was interested in only one man.

Continuing to respond to their conversation with smiling and suggestive quips, Samantha glanced around her. She noted that Helen and Jim Sutton sat at a table in the corner. Although Jim still was one of her regulars, he now spent his spare time with Helen. The quiet brunette seemed to be his confidante in matters that he wouldn't otherwise discuss, and she was glad. She apparently had done something right, although she seemed to have done everything else wrong.

Samantha nursed an inner anger, concealed since Matt had left her unexpectedly in the alleyway a week earlier. Unlike Toby, who continued to warn her against the path she was taking, the fellas surrounding her still didn't realize her true focus.

Samantha was disturbed by that thought. She knew what she had come to Winston to do, but she wasn't comfortable with her unanticipated feelings for Matt. She had been overwhelmed by the emotion that he had stirred in that alleyway. She had intentionally conveyed those feelings—of course— yet the scope of her response had not been planned.

The image of Matt leaving her abruptly still rankled. She could not avoid the truth that she had watched the doorway during the days since, getting angrier by the minute when he did not appear. She had determined when she awoke that morning that if he didn't show up that day, she would take steps of her own.

"What, no welcome?"

Samantha turned to see the object of her mental meanderings standing behind her. Stunned, she looked up into the face that had filled her dreams throughout otherwise sleepless nights; yet she felt nothing at all.

Matt continued with an easy charm. "I want to apologize for leaving you so abruptly a week ago. I've been hoping we can take up where we left off without too much difficulty."

Samantha could not find her voice. Not only had Matt surprised her, but he was almost . . . *cloying!* She had previously been so sensitive to Matt that she could feel his arrival the moment he walked through the doorway. Now as she perused his face, her gaze lingering on the contours of the strong features and full lips that used to set her heart pounding, she realized that the former barrier he had purposely erected between them appeared to have dissipated.

But so had the magic.

Samantha's other admirers reluctantly melted away. Bemused by her sudden lack of feeling for the man standing before her, she told herself that she was relieved to be free of the emotional entanglement. Frowning, she discovered that she was actually annoyed when Matt sought to caress her intimately.

She reacted hotly. "Wait a minute. Last week you left me just when things were getting interesting between us."

Matt shrugged. "That was not one of my better decisions."

"One of your *better decisions*?"

"I decided to walk away then, but I've been doing some thinking about it in the time since. I made a mistake. I'm here to correct it."

"I've also been doing some thinking. I figure it might be time to change some things, too."

"It's always dangerous for a woman to think."

"Is that so?" Silently outraged, Samantha replied with tenuous control, "I've done a lot of thinking most of my life. I hate to believe I've been wasting my time."

"All I can say to that is . . ." Matt paused to revise his intended response. "If thinking brought you to me right now, I have to figure it wasn't wasted."

Oh, he was too smooth!

Samantha gritted her teeth and smiled forcibly. She didn't like Matt's attitude or the way the conversation between them was progressing. As a matter of fact, she didn't like Matt.

Realizing that last acknowledgment could cause her a problem, Samantha said, "Look, things got a little out of control that day for both of us. I think we should start again and get to know each other a little better."

Matt leaned closer to trail his mouth against her cheek. He whispered, "I think we know each other well enough already."

"I don't." Aware that Matt was about to cover her mouth with his, Samantha ordered coldly, "Not so fast."

Matt did not reply.

"I have some pride, you know."

"If you had *pride,* you wouldn't be working here."

Samantha bristled. "As far as I'm concerned, you're going to have to make up for that fiasco in the alleyway a week ago."

"I was only joking with my last remark," Matt replied belatedly.

"You weren't funny."

"Maybe not. I'm sorry."

Somehow even angrier, Samantha said, "I don't want to end up like I did last week. I need to know what to expect from you. We need to talk."

Matt drew back, his light eyes hardening. "Talking isn't exactly what I had in mind."

"Maybe so, but I didn't have a deserted alleyway as my ultimate goal when I first saw you, either. Just so you know," Samantha continued, "there are plenty of fellas willing to take your place right now, so I need to make something clear. I expect some conversation first."

"Conversation."

"Considering what happened, I need to know a little about you . . . about the way you think."

"You know all you need to know."

"But not all that I intend to know, especially why you left me that day."

"I told you—"

"You said you made a bad decision, but you didn't say why."

Samantha realized the risk she was taking when Matt drew himself up angrily and said, "I guess it's time for me to think some things over, too. You're obviously not the woman I believed you were."

"Is that good or bad?"

"I'll let you know."

Turning away from her without another word, he strode back across the saloon and out through the swinging doors.

Once again left abandoned and seething, Samantha was determined not to show anger when a voice at her elbow said, "It's not like I didn't warn you."

Samantha turned toward Toby and replied automatically, "He's a bastard, but I'll figure him out."

"If you'll take off those blinders you're wearing, I think it'll be pretty obvious what Matt is thinking."

Samantha looked at the old man's sober expression. She knew what his reply would be before she asked, "And what is that?"

"Matt figures it's worth spending some time with you, but not his whole future."

"What if I'm not interested in the future, either?" Samantha replied deliberately.

"If you're not, you're doing a damned good imitation of wanting more than Matt's willing to offer."

"I only asked for some conversation."

"He don't want it."

"I don't care what he wants. It's what *I* want that counts."

"Then look for another fella."

"What if I don't want to?"

"Well, then . . ." Toby's lined face screwed up with concern. "I guess you have to come to a compromise with what you want and with what Matt is willing to give. There's nothing else to do, other than to forget him entirely."

"You're telling me I can't have it both ways."

"Right."

"You're wrong." Resolved, Samantha said with conviction, "And I'm going to prove it—when I figure out how."

"You're a determined woman, do you know that? I'm starting to think maybe Matt made a mistake when he chose Jenny over you." He shrugged. "But in any case, I'd like to keep you company until you straighten all this out in your head. If that's all right with you, of course."

Somehow unable to resist the old man, Samantha said, "It's all right with me. I've discovered that I actually enjoy your company, no matter what you say, Toby."

"I know you do."

Samantha replied with sudden sincerity, "Damn it all! If you were only twenty years younger."

"Thirty years is more like it." Turning to the mustached bartender, Toby said more loudly, "The lady and me would like a drink when you get a chance." He added, "As a matter of fact, leave the bottle."

Toby carried it to a nearby table a few minutes later, Samantha close behind. She had a genuine affection for the old man.

But she still did not understand the bastard named Matt Strait.

Helen and Jim watched the proceedings between Samantha and Matt silently. They then watched as Samantha and Toby made their way to a table. They exchanged glances and shook their heads.

The sky was dark and so was most of Main Street hours later when Samantha walked unsteadily beside Lola, Paulette, and Helen toward the Sleepy Rest Hotel. Maggie and Denise had left the Trail's End with their male friends of the hour, which they were prone to do. No one was surprised.

The saloon women all lived in the less than desirable rooms at the Sleepy Rest, the town's only hotel. The lodgings there were designed for transients and for people like them who did not live in the more respectable houses on First Street. The same could be said for the small restaurant next door, where offerings were neither extensive nor good.

Showing his age, Toby had gone back to his room behind the livery stable to sleep off the effects of an empty bottle, leaving Samantha to spend the remainder of the evening fending off the amorous advances of drunken cowboys. She had congratulated herself on being able to hold her liquor, but she suddenly realized when she staggered unexpectedly that she wasn't as sober as she had thought she was.

Samantha grunted in a totally unladylike manner and quickened her step to keep up with the girls. She realized suddenly that they were more sober than she was, and that thought upset her. She didn't like the failure in personal judgment that admission represented. It wasn't professional. She was glad Allan Pinkerton wasn't there to see her.

"I've been waiting to talk to you, Samantha."

Samantha's step faltered when a shadow materialized into Matt's unexpected figure. She raised her chin to scrutinize him more carefully. She stared at his handsome face, wondering why she had been so drawn to him. It wasn't as if she had never seen a man as big and masculine as he was before. Or as handsome.

He towered over her, waiting for her to speak, and she stared at him a second longer. He was still as big and muscular and all male as he had been, but the magic had disappeared, all right. She told herself again that she was glad—but she wasn't so sure.

She had some sober thinking to do.

Paulette and Lola said almost in unison, "I'll see you tomorrow, Samantha." They grasped Helen's arm as she seemed ready to disagree and pulled her along with them.

Samantha turned unsteadily. "No, don't go."

Helen looked back at her as Paulette and Lola dragged her along toward the hotel.

Frowning, Samantha turned back to Matt. She said with a hiccup, "What . . . what do you want?"

"I want to talk to you." Matt smiled, but she had the feeling his smile did not come from the heart when he said, "But I think you could use some help getting to your room, too."

"Why, because I've had too . . . too much to drink?" Samantha silently cursed when she hiccupped again. She raised her chin a notch higher. "As you can see, now is not the time to talk."

Taking her arm, Matt said, "Talking isn't all I had in mind for tonight."

"What did you have in mind?" Samantha shook off his grip as she stood swaying in the middle of the street. "If you think you can just take up where we left off in that alleyway, you're mistaken."

"I just want to see you to your room."

"Yeah." Samantha nodded with a lopsided smile. "Really."

"I don't believe you. As a matter of fact, I don't believe a word you say!"

Matt shrugged again. "You're the one who wanted to get to know me better."

31

Samantha drew back, her gaze narrowing. "Yes, by *talking*!"

"Talking, huh?"

"That's right."

"Well, this is your chance."

"No, it isn't. I wanted to know what to expect from you, but I already know what to expect from you tonight."

"Maybe you do and maybe you don't." Matt stepped closer. His gaze hardened as did a more obvious part of him as he took her arm again. His grip was harsher and his belated smile did not ring true when he began, "I only want to make sure—"

Aware that he was stronger and more determined than she was, Samantha suddenly knew she had no recourse. Reaching down with her other hand, she lifted her skirt to withdraw the small derringer concealed in a holster on her thigh. Matt went still when he saw the small gun and heard her warn, "I don't want to use this gun on you. I've never needed to use it before, but I'm telling you now that I won't hesitate."

Matt released her arm. All pretense at a smile disappeared when he said, "You don't want to do that, Samantha."

"You're right, I don't. But I will. So get on that horse of yours and ride out of town—and I'll go to sleep like I want to."

She hiccupped again.

Matt smiled engagingly. "I'll give you a last

chance to change your mind. I know you'll be sorry if you don't."

"I won't be sorry and I won't change my mind— not tonight, anyway." She frowned when she said with unexpected honesty, "Tomorrow, maybe."

"I'm not promising there'll be a tomorrow for us."

Samantha whispered, "Then I'll just have to take that chance, won't I? Get moving!"

Samantha saw the look in Matt's light eyes then. Frustrated and angry he mumbled, "I'm warning you—"

"Git!"

Her finger tightened on the trigger and Matt turned abruptly toward the horse he had tethered at a nearby rail. He mounted stiffly without looking back and rode out of town.

Left in the dust of his departure, Samantha waited until Matt turned the bend in the street. She coughed and then hiccupped again before continuing toward the hotel. She needed rest, all right. She needed to be able to think clearly. She had come to Winston to get proof of Matt's involvement in the robberies, hadn't she? So what had changed?

Samantha closed the hotel room door behind her minutes later, locked it, and lit the bedside lamp. Staring at her image in the mottled dresser mirror across from her, she asked aloud, "What in hell did I get myself into?"

She then flopped onto the bed, that question un-answered as she immediately fell asleep.

* * *

The sunbeams of late morning assaulted Samantha with a violence she had never before experienced. Rising with a throbbing head and a sick stomach, she had little interest in dressing her part when she started down the stairs. So great was her discomfort that she had been unable to apply her saloon makeup carefully or complete her toilette. Her scalp had been so tender that she had not bothered to put up her hair, but had left it streaming down over her shoulders in a modest hairstyle that contrasted severely with the voluptuous afternoon gown she had bought for her saloon-woman masquerade.

Arriving at the bottom of the staircase, she squinted against the pounding headache that had not relented and ignored the knowing glances that came her way. Samantha knew she was not at her best. She figured she was suffering for her mistakes of the previous night, and her mind was on the restaurant where she hoped she could get some coffee to survive the nausea that threatened.

But first she needed some air.

Samantha emerged out onto the street, the question that had gone unanswered when she fell asleep the previous night still haunting her.

What in hell had she gotten herself into?

She wondered briefly if she had made a mistake by chasing off Matt, especially when he had obviously waited hours for her the previous night. It took her only a second to confirm in her mind that she hadn't. He had not wanted to talk. The sticky problem was that she hadn't wanted to talk, either—or to do anything but sleep.

It occurred to her then that she had wanted no part of him, in strange contrast with her first breathless attraction.

She shook her head. He was . . . he was—

Samantha went still. He was crossing the street! He was also nodding in response to the plain young woman he was holding possessively by the arm. The young woman was conversing with him in a manner that was too familiar to suit Samantha.

Conversing with the other woman when he had no intention of conversing with her.

Possessively holding the other woman's arm when his attentions to her were admittedly only temporary.

That other woman could be no one but his fiancée, Jenny Morgan.

Samantha realized that she concurred with Toby. Jenny wasn't much to look at.

Matt glanced up at that moment. Their gazes met and a silent heat stirred again in the pit of Samantha's stomach.

Astounded by her jealous anger when Matt acknowledged her only with a nod before deliberately tucking Jenny's arm more firmly under his and stepping out of sight in the mercantile, Samantha gasped. Infuriated, she approached the store. She waited outside, shaking, uncertain exactly what she intended and hoping to gain control before she did something she would regret. Yet her heart was still pounding when Matt emerged a few minutes later and stopped still at the sight of her.

Pulling him farther down the walk and into the shadows of a building, Samantha demanded, "What do you have to say for yourself?"

Matt responded with a coldness that did not reach the passion in his gaze. "I think I made myself clear the last time I saw you."

"I agree. You did."

"What's that supposed to mean? I told you how I feel." Matt took a step closer. She saw his eyes travel her flushed expression and saw the spontaneous hunger he suppressed when his gaze touched her lips.

Matt's reluctant desire resounded inside her. Her mouth going dry, Samantha retreated as she whispered, "You're telling me that if I had let you take me up to my hotel room last night, you'd be a different man today? You're saying that it would be my arm you'd be holding so possessively and my conversation you'd be acknowledging?" She laughed harshly. "I don't think so."

"Last night I—"

"Last night you what? You wanted me, but you wanted me on your terms?"

Matt did not speak.

"You won't answer me, will you?" Samantha took a breath, suddenly aware that she was close to tears. She could deny it no longer. The magic between them had returned even stronger than before and she was at its mercy. Unable to understand Matt, but knowing she desperately wanted to, she was certain of only one thing. She blurted out her thoughts in a trembling voice.

"You didn't want to talk to me in the alleyway last week, and you didn't want to talk to me last night. But if I hadn't pulled my gun on you, you'd be lying in my bed right now with no thought of your fiancée."

Matt blinked.

"Isn't that right?"

No response.

"Isn't it?"

Following Matt's gaze, Samantha saw Jenny hesitate at the doorway of the mercantile before walking back inside for something she had obviously forgotten. Pain surged hotly inside her when Matt took a step back farther into the shadows where Jenny could not see him.

Her chin rose defiantly. "I can see you're worried that your *fiancée* might see us together. You don't want that, do you? You can't be honest with either her or me!"

"Samantha—"

"Don't worry. I won't tell her—not unless you don't come to the Trail's End tonight so we can talk. *Talk*, do you understand? I won't have a repetition of what happened last night!"

Silent, his only reaction the tightening of his jaw

and a look in his light eyes that she did not quite comprehend, Matt turned back toward the mercantile without a word in response.

She raised her voice to say, "I expect to see you tonight at the Trail's End!"

Arriving at the doorway just as Jenny emerged, Matt took her arm and left Samantha standing in the shadows—*alone again*.

Another evening found Samantha standing in a circle of determined admirers at the Trail's End, but she was inwardly shaking. She reacted to that emotion with a sharpening of witty repartee, while inwardly wondering how long she would be able to use her quick mind to escape the intentions of the amorous group.

An inner sense slowly turning her, Samantha saw Matt standing at the swinging doors. Her admirers left her reluctantly when they saw her expression, and Samantha swallowed tightly. She then heard the single remaining member of that group speak up in warning.

"Remember what I said, Samantha. Matt's not the man for you." A note of surrender entered Toby's voice a few moments later when he added, "But I guess we all have to make our own mistakes."

Samantha acknowledged somewhere in the back of her mind that Toby's warning made sense, but his sage advice had no affect on the familiar quivering inside her. She did not try to stop him from leaving as Matt approached with an expression proving he was no more successful than she in hiding the emotions that ran hot and cold between them.

Samantha knew, however, that in allowing her feelings to get out of hand, she had behaved more like a jealous shrew than the professional investigator she hoped to be. With that thought in mind, Samantha forced herself to remember that Matt was a criminal—a criminal she hoped to bring to justice.

She said succinctly, "So you came."

"Did I have a choice?"

"Yes, you did." Suddenly angry, she said, "You could have told your precious fiancée how you behaved in the alleyway that afternoon."

"That wasn't entirely my fault."

"And how you behaved last night? Or wasn't that your fault, either?"

"Last night—I can't take full blame for that."

"Really? Just tell me, then, who am I to believe— the fellow who left me alone in the alleyway last week, the fellow I had to pull a gun on in order to make him leave last night, or the fellow who is here right now?"

"I only came here tonight because you threatened me."

"Now tell me another one."

Matt suddenly demanded, "I'm not going to let you ruin everything I've worked for."

"What do you mean?"

Matt's jaw locked tight. "I'll be able to pay off the debts on the ranch my pa left me soon. Then I'll marry Jenny."

Matt's statement cut deep and Samantha responded, "Your plain little wren, you mean?"

"Jenny is a good woman and a good friend."

"Is she a good lover, too?"

Matt's jaw tensed.

"I asked you a question."

"I don't choose to answer it."

"You don't make love to her, do you?" Inexplicably relieved when the truth became suddenly clear, Samantha whispered, "You don't even have the desire to make love to her."

"I love Jenny. She's a good friend and she'll make me a good wife."

"Do you love her?"

"I do."

"But do you *want her*?" Samantha stared up into Matt's darkening expression. Her voice dropped a note softer as she insisted, "Let me be more specific. Do you want her as much as you want me?"

Color flooded Matt's face. His lips moved with a silent curse before he whispered, "I warned you before that you're playing with fire."

"You didn't answer my question."

Waiting interminably before responding, Matt said softly, "I thought you wanted me to come here so we could talk."

"We are talking."

"You're talking, but I don't intend to answer."

"I'm making sense. You just don't want to admit that I am."

"Samantha, I'm warning you—"

"About what?"

Matt's gaze seared her to the bone. Suddenly certain that she would have given herself to him at that moment without another word, Samantha watched incredulously as Matt turned abruptly and strode toward the door.

Disbelief flooded Samantha's mind.

Reality dawned.

She didn't want him to leave. Instead, she wanted—

Refusing to finish that thought as Matt walked through the swinging doors and stepped out of sight on the street beyond, Samantha turned slowly back to the bar.

Another long night over at last, Samantha walked silently beside Lola, Helen, and Paulette as they headed toward their rooms at the Sleepy Rest. The town was all but dark in the early hours of morning, and she was tired.

"I wish Denise and Maggie realized those cowboys are just taking them for what they can get."

Helen's comments raised Lola's eyebrows. Only a few years older than Helen but wiser in experience, the redhead replied, "Did it ever occur to you that maybe Maggie and Denise are taking those cowboys for all *they* can get?"

Helen was silent and Samantha felt a moment's pity. The young brunette still believed in true love. Helen was still certain she would meet the man of her dreams in that bar someday and marry him.

Samantha realized that she had formerly been as sure of the future as Helen was. She had believed that she would recognize the man of her dreams the moment she saw him, and he would love her as much as she loved him. Then she had met Matt, and everything she believed in had been turned upside down.

She reminded herself again that Matt was a criminal, that she hoped to become a Pinkerton, and that those facts were incompatible with her feelings.

Samantha trudged onward. She was stone-cold sober. She had learned her lesson. She also needed a clear mind to be able to think things through and she—

"You win, Samantha."

Samantha stopped short as a figure stepped out of the shadows to stand towering over her as she neared the hotel. The other women hurried toward the hotel without speaking a word, dragging Helen along with them. She stood motionless as Matt walked closer. She scrutinized the height and breadth of him; the thick, dark hair underneath his weathered Stetson; the light eyes that were at present earnest; the strong features; and the generous mouth that had raised such wild longings inside her.

Samantha's heartbeat escalated as Matt whispered, "I told myself that I came to see you tonight so we could talk. That sounded reasonable. I figured I needed to explain some things, but everything changed when I saw you. You're right, you know. I never made love to Jenny because I never wanted her the way I want you. And the truth is that I want you now more than I have any right to want you. You're all I've thought about since I first met you. I'm not certain what that means, but—"

Interrupting, Samantha said honestly, "I'm not certain what that means, either. I just know one thing."

Matt waited for her to continue.

In a voice hoarse with passion, Samantha whispered with sudden certainty, "I know that whatever these feelings do mean, Matt—I'm yours."

Time moved swiftly as soon as Matt closed the door of Samantha's small hotel room. Heated by their passion, the room sweltered as lips mingled and hands struggled with the impediment of clothing until naked flesh touched.

Matt stifled a groan at the first contact with Samantha's bare skin. His ardor rebounded inside Samantha as he moved instinctively, sending her senses reeling.

She accommodated his seeking mouth and his

kiss sank deeper. His tongue caressed hers. He tasted and explored the aching flesh she offered him and her heartbeat thundered with a hunger she could no longer deny.

Their hunger intensified. The sweat of mutual fervor bound them.

Samantha gasped when Matt took her breasts into his mouth. Her need became a mindless hunger that matched his when he tasted them at last. She wrapped her fingers in his hair to clutch him tight against her.

The hunger heightened.

The need accelerated.

Their gasps were simultaneous when he entered her at last.

Samantha wrapped her legs around him, drawing him closer to join his penetrating plunges, raising herself so he might sink more deeply inside her, exhilarating in the moment with a frenzy that she did not recognize as her own.

Colors flashed before her closed eyelids as their lovemaking became red-hot.

Samantha held her breath as climax neared—but Matt paused. He looked down at her, his gaze passionate yet suddenly uncertain.

Why was he waiting? She loved him. Hadn't she proved that to him? He was everything she had ever wanted, everything she had ever needed. They were meant for each other

Or—were they?

Then came the ultimate question: Was this the solution she had been seeking?

Knowing she could not deny those uncertainties, and knowing that Matt suffered them as well, Samantha was suddenly aware that she needed to speak the words Matt waited to hear.

Unable to think past the moment, Samantha whispered hoarsely, "Make love to me, Matt. Make love to me, and I promise that I will make love to you, too."

His light eyes revealing more than words could convey, Matt whispered an unintelligible word with his final thrust.

The world rocked!

Colors exploded!

A shared throbbing ecstasy burst forth to seal the moment in time.

Samantha clutched Matt closer as they soared together to fulfillment. She held him tight against her until his strong body stilled and her own was motionless as well.

Samantha felt Matt raise his head at last to look down into her impassioned expression. Reluctant to release her, he whispered against her mouth, "I will never be able to get enough of you."

She responded instinctively, wordlessly, accepting the homage of his lips when he offered them. She felt his body swell anew inside her as his kiss sank deeper. Her need renewed, she rejoiced as the momentum of his stroking increased.

And then—she rose higher! She flew more freely! She had not believed the second time could be better than the first, or that Matt's lovemaking could renew the kaleidoscope of sensations inside her that were so recently spent.

She lay motionless in his arms minutes later and breathed deeply. It was so right.

Wasn't it?

Waiting long moments after his body shuddered again to a halt atop Samantha, Matt lifted himself to scrutinize her face. She was so beautiful. Her perfect, naked length glowed a pale silhouette in the darkness of the room. Her loosened hair stretched across the pillow in a golden trail that was his alone. The thick fringe of brown lashes lay against her flawless cheeks, and her mouth—the moist, giving wonder of it—lay only inches from his.

She was his alone, just as she had said.

Incredulous, Matt realized that the words he had spoken were truer than he realized. He could never get enough of Samantha. He wanted her still—not only her body, but also the warmth of her, her instinctive generosity of spirit, and the acceptance she had demonstrated despite her many uncertainties.

Matt saw Samantha's eyelids stir. She opened them and he saw the emotion in the hazel depths of her eyes.

But those depths were shadowed like his own.

He whispered, "All I can say to you right now is

that you fill my mind and heart more than I had thought possible."

He saw the hesitation in Samantha's expression. Those were not the words she had hoped to hear. Yet he knew instinctively that he shouldn't attempt to straighten out all the things that had gone haywire in the past few weeks during the intimacy of that moment.

Feeling a familiar desire stir inside him, Matt looked down at Samantha. He mused again that she was so perfect in his arms . . . so beautiful, so instinctive, so . . . honest. She was far too good to settle for the life she had set for herself.

Still joined to her, Matt drew Samantha closer and rested his lips against her cheek. She lay unmoving underneath him, a part of him.

Matt slid his mouth along her cheek in a trail to her parted lips. She *was* a part of him—an intimate and necessary part—and he owed her more than she had been given.

He would settle everything tomorrow. But for tonight, for whatever time remained, she belonged to him.

Chapter Three

Samantha awoke slowly. Her body ached, a personal pain that was pleasure indeed. She remembered—

Samantha snapped her eyes open wide to find morning sunlight streaming through the hotel window's tattered blinds. The bed beside her was empty.

She was momentarily at a loss. Had she imagined the previous night? Had it actually happened, or was it a dream? Had she allowed Matt to make love to her again and again—as if he were a lover and not a criminal whom she had come to Winston to hunt down?

Yet his scent still lingered in the room and her body bore the sweet aching of a woman who had been adored thoroughly and completely until exhaustion prevailed.

Momentarily confused, Samantha shook her head. She could not have made up such vivid feelings. Matt had worshipped her body in ways she had never dreamed, and she had responded instinctively to his touch.

But where was he now?

Samantha recalled belatedly that she had opened her eyes while it was still dark to see Matt dressing in the shadows. Exhaustion had claimed her consciousness then. All she could remember afterward was the click of the hallway door when it had closed behind him.

Fully awake now, Samantha searched the room for a note explaining Matt's abrupt departure. She ignored her nakedness when she stood beside the dresser mirror and saw a note in a scrawling, masculine hand.

It read:

Last night was a privilege I do not fully deserve. Thank you.

Matt

Samantha stood with the note in hand, incredulous that she had been abandoned again.

Would she never learn?

With considerable care and steadfast determination, Samantha washed all trace of Matt from her body. Toby's whispered comments seemed all the timelier:

"Any interest you might stir up in him won't be for the long run." And later, *"I'm thinking you're not as world-wise as you make out to be."*

Toby had been right all along. She had somehow believed that her feelings for Matt were strong enough to conquer all uncertainty. She had surrendered to the powerful emotions he raised in her, but she now regretted her lapse for more reasons than she cared to count.

Samantha frowned at her use of the word *surrender*. Surrender of any kind boded poorly for the professional life she intended—which was her ultimate goal. She would not make the same mistake again.

The pain of reality overwhelming, Samantha forced herself to think clinically as she dressed. She reviewed the information that had set her on Matt's trail. Most condemning of all for Matt were the positive identifications of several bank employees. But Matt had an alibi verified by others during every robbery.

The questions remaining were:

Was it arrogance that had caused her not to recognize that Matt was clever—perhaps cleverer than she?

Why had she not acknowledged that Matt could appear innocent and truthful while being guilty of robbing banks?

Was it because Matt's ardor during the night past was difficult to question that she had believed it was not a passing fancy on his part?

Dressed and her final assessment completed, Samantha knew the answer to all those questions.

Matt had never said the three words she had longed to hear. She was determined that his lack of pretense would enable her to put her brief lapse behind her.

Sufficiently cleansed and fortified, Samantha then started toward the street for breakfast. She had little appetite, but she would not allow a night of passion to affect her. She had learned a severe lesson. It was all part of the game.

And she intended to be strong enough to play it.

Matt rode at a brisk canter along the wilderness trail as the sky lightened with morning. He had arisen from Samantha's bed at daybreak and had glanced at her sleeping face. The truth was that he had not regretted the night past. How could he, with the memory of rapture still vivid and the aching desire to recapture those moments still keen?

Yet his conscience tormented him. Jenny was his fiancée. He had known her all his life and had made a commitment to her. And even if he did not have the same desire for her that he did for Samantha, he did truly love her.

Another truth was that he had become aware of Samantha the first moment he walked into the Trail's End. With awareness had come an ever-expanding desire that Samantha seemed to share. He knew the danger she presented to him from that moment on. He had promised himself after their first encounter that he would avoid her, but an offhanded remark that she made during their conversation had caused him to visit her again.

Uncertain if that last thought was completely true, Matt admitted that the end result was that Samantha's scent now teased him, the remembered taste of her taunted him, and instead of diminishing, his desire for her had increased.

His mind in turmoil, Matt was sure of only one thing. He would take care of something that he had already avoided too long.

The sun had fully risen when Matt drew up a cautious distance from the isolated cabin he sought. Dismounting, he withdrew his gun and silently advanced. The cabin appeared abandoned and silent, but a horse ate casually in a shelter behind the cabin.

Matt took a deep breath. It was now or never.

Bursting through the doorway with his gun drawn, Matt halted when he came face-to-face with the barrel of another gun—*and with a man who was the mirror image of himself!*

His chest heaving, Matt growled heatedly, "You're a bastard, Tucker!"

"Right, that's what I am. I guess that's what we both are, *brother.*"

Matt stared at his twin. The thought flashed through his mind, as it had often since discovering the existence of his brother a few years earlier, that if it had been he instead of Tucker whom their irresponsible, self-serving mother had decided to take with her when she left their father, *he* might now be the wanted man.

Hardly conscious of the moment their guns were simultaneously lowered, Matt advanced toward Tucker Conroy.

Tucker viewed his *older* brother coldly as he walked toward him. They were a mirror image of each other, all right. Even he could not believe how identical their appearances were. The rugged cut of their thick black hair was the same, and the dark brows over light eyes were identical, as were the planes of face, mouth, and chin. Although their lifestyles were entirely different, even their physiques were alike.

Yet Matt was *the chosen one*, the elder of the two by a few minutes. He was the firstborn of his father's identical twin sons, and the son his father had decided to keep.

Tucker said abruptly, "I have a few questions I've waited a long time to ask, so here goes, brother. Exactly why are you here now when you never sought me out before?"

"I avoided you at first, just as you avoided me, I suppose," Matt replied coolly.

"Why? You're Jeremy Strait's son. He kept you when he ran our mother and me off."

"Ran you both off?" Matt shook his head. "You don't really believe that, do you? Our mother ran off when the going got tough. She only took you with her because she figured you would be her way back in if she decided to return."

"That's not what she told me."

Matt sneered. "And you believed her."

Tucker took an aggressive step forward, anger clear in the planes of his handsome face. "Our mother did the best she could with what she had— which was very little thanks to Jeremy Strait."

"Lies, all of it."

"I'm the proof."

"I suppose that's true." Momentarily saddened, Matt asked, "Why does it surprise you that our mother wasn't what she pretended to be? She refused to marry our father even though she was pregnant."

"Jeremy Strait never wanted to marry her!"

Matt did not respond.

A smile so like Matt's briefly curved Tucker's lips when he said, "Would it surprise you that when our mother told me you existed shortly before her death, I tried to find you? My efforts stopped when I discovered our father had allowed everyone to believe you were his only son and that he had declared you his sole beneficiary."

"As far as Pa knew, I *was* his only son and sole heir to his bankrupt ranch. The only thing of value he left me was the sterling silver belt buckle that he wore. He promised it to me when I was a child because I admired the longhorn carving on it. He told me about you on his deathbed and said he didn't even know if you and our mother were both still alive."

"But he didn't try to find me through all those years, did he?"

"He was too busy trying to raise an infant son and working from dawn to dusk trying to save the ranch our mother had helped drive into debt."

"I don't believe you."

"You wouldn't."

Suddenly angry, Tucker said hotly, "It all turned out quite well, though, when that secret worked unexpectedly to my advantage. I took the opportunity and used it well."

"Everything you did was deliberate, then," Matt said incredulously.

"Sure it was deliberate! I don't think the same way you do, brother. I left whatever home our mother provided as soon as I came of age, even though I kept track of her and found her whenever she was destitute. She never asked what I was doing or where the money I gave her came from, and it's just as well. When I returned the last time, she had been drunk and hit by a runaway carriage. She was dying, but she told me about you first."

"So you used our identical appearances to confound the law."

"I figured being your twin had to be good for something," Tucker said sarcastically.

"Bastard!"

"I confess it amused me that you could easily have set matters straight by confessing that you had a twin brother. I wondered how long it would take for you to cave in to the pressure I created."

"I haven't caved in yet."

"Because you don't want to admit that you have a twin brother who might have a legal claim to your sole inheritance!"

"You know that's not the reason!"

"What is it, then?"

Matt mumbled under his breath, "If you don't know, it won't do any good for me to tell you." He took a breath and continued in a more threatening tone. "But I'm here to say something I should have said before."

"It wouldn't have anything to do with your *saloon woman*, would it, brother?"

Matt flushed. "Samantha Rigg is not my saloon woman, but she's not yours, either."

"I admit that the rumors about your encounter with Samantha were music to my ears. It showed me that you're not really what you pretend to be, just like our father."

"Don't talk about our father. You don't know what he was really like."

"That's not my fault." Waiting until that gibe struck home, Tucker continued. "But dear Jenny doesn't know anything about Samantha, does she? You were always so faithful to her in the past that she doesn't even have a suspicion. That reason alone made me determined to meet the woman who had finally penetrated your defenses. I have to admit that my visit to Samantha wasn't a full success, but it did bring you to me with a gun in your hand."

Matt took a menacing step forward, and Tucker raised his gun. "That's far enough."

"I want to make something clear." Matt's voice—so similar to Tucker's—dropped a note lower as he warned, "I don't care what you do with your life, as long as you don't interfere with mine. That means I don't want you pretending to be me with Samantha. She's off-limits."

"Why?"

Ignoring the gun pointed in his direction as well as his brother's question, Matt took another menacing step. "Just stay away from Samantha."

Tucker remained silent.

"You didn't answer me."

"I'm thinking it over."

Matt took another step forward and Tucker laughed out loud, stopping Matt in his tracks. "All right, it's a bargain. No more contact with Samantha. All right?"

"How do I know you'll keep your word?"

"You'll have to trust me, brother," Tucker replied.

Matt did not respond and Tucker's expression hardened.

"So, if you've said all you came here to say, you can walk back out that door now."

"Listen, bastard—" Matt began.

"No, you listen!" Suddenly angry, Tucker said hotly, "I've been the younger brother all my life without knowing it, but I don't intend to let you take advantage of that accident of birth now. I'll do whatever I please, so get out!"

"Not before I've made myself clear."

"Don't threaten me."

"I'm not threatening you. I'm telling you. If you know what's good for you, you'll keep your word and stay away from Samantha. You won't contact her in any way, do you understand?"

"So protective . . ."

Matt stared at his twin. A part of him was incredulous that his father had managed to keep Tucker's existence a secret for so many years. Another part of him despised the mirror image that stared back at him belligerently.

A deadening guilt stirred. He had gotten the better end of the bargain, and he knew it. Tucker was admittedly guilty of bank robbery but was enjoying safety from Texas law because of Matt. He detested being used, but he could not bring himself to turn his brother in.

But in trying to seduce Samantha, Tucker had gone too far.

Matt reiterated with growing menace, "I'm warning you for the last time—stay away from Samantha, or brother or not, you'll live to regret it."

Turning toward the door before Tucker could reply, Matt strode outside and mounted his horse. He rode away from the cabin hoping he would never need to return.

* * *

Tucker watched as his twin turned on his heel and left, slamming the cabin door behind him.

Silent until the sound of Matt's horse faded into the distance, Tucker grew suddenly enraged. His voice echoed in the empty cabin as he said, "Don't worry, Matt. I won't break my word and visit Samantha again, but I'll prove that, contrary to our father's belief, *you're no better than I am.*"

Tucker smiled unexpectedly, his expression taking on a light totally unlike his brother's as he continued. "Strangely, you didn't mention Jenny. Dear Jenny. Plain Jenny. Sweet and innocent Jenny."

Tucker paused, his expression hardening. "I think it's time the two of us became acquainted."

Chapter Four

Jenny walked slowly along Winston's main street. Traffic was beginning to stir with the new day. She had left her pa at the ranch with the excuse she needed supplies from the mercantile, a lie that she had felt was necessary to tell.

Jenny tied up her wagon and stepped down onto the boardwalk. She touched the thick brown hair she wore in a bun underneath her plain straw hat. She frowned at the sunshine that filtered down onto her fair, ordinary features. She had always known she was plain. Brown hair, brown eyes, undistinguished features, and slim beyond fashion, she had even taken to wearing plain cottons that suited her totally ordinary appearance.

She had decided earlier in life that her role had been defined for her before she was born. She was the daughter of Randolph Morgan, who had raised her lovingly and the best way he knew after her mother died in childbirth. She had assumed housekeeping duties at their ranch as soon as she was able, and she knew that the possible joining of Matt's and their land when her father was too old to run his own ranch gave him great comfort. She was grateful she could afford her father that much, since she could afford nothing else.

Yet she was so plain, and Matt was so handsome.

Jenny recalled with a tinge of guilt the first time she met Matt, when she was eight years old. Always thin, small, and timid, she was picked on mercilessly by the bullies in their one-room schoolhouse. Forced to run and hide during recess rather than be considered a tattletale by others, she had bumped into the tall, already good-looking older boy who had demanded unexpectedly, "Don't you ever get tired of running away? Why don't you fight back?"

Jenny had never forgotten the questions Matt had asked her—just as she had never forgotten him. With that question ringing in her mind, she had nervously faced down her tormentors afterward. When they eventually gave up tormenting her, she had felt powerful without having exerted any physical effort at all. She knew she had used Matt's strength when her own was lacking, but she had felt no guilt. Matt had stimulated courage in her with his simple questions. She valued it, just as she valued him.

"You trust too easily, Jenny."

Mary Sears, her friend since childhood, had made that inexplicable comment the previous day. Mary had appeared reluctant to say more, but those words had struck a chord because she had noticed a change in Matt recently. Matt had begun avoiding direct contact with her gaze and appeared averse to discuss their future. Since theirs was a friendship of years, she had known instinctively that something was wrong. Mary's words, whether they revealed a hidden jealousy or not, only confirmed her thoughts.

"Aren't you tired of running away? Why don't you fight back?"

Matt's comments from years earlier rang again in her mind. She was determined he would never have to ask those questions again.

Stopping still, Jenny saw the woman she was seeking emerge from the hotel. Samantha Rigg hesitated on the walk, but even gaudily dressed and heavily painted, Jenny realized she was beautiful.

Jenny took a deep breath and approached her directly. She halted a few feet from the beauteous saloon girl, remembering Matt's angry question.

Yes, she was tired of running away.

Samantha came face-to-face with a plain young woman with a resolute expression. Her heart pounded. She knew who the woman was, yet anger and guilt competed in her mind as she waited for Jenny to speak.

"I know who you are. You're Samantha Rigg. My name is Jenny Morgan, and you know why I'm here." Her face flushing a pale red, Jenny began slowly.

"This is a small town. It doesn't take long for everyone to hear stories that are circulating. I've heard the stories about Matt and you. I know he is attracted to you and you to him. Seeing you now, I can understand why. You're both extraordinarily pleasant to look at and you seemingly deserve each other."

Pausing to swallow, Jenny continued. "But the truth is just the opposite. Matt doesn't deserve a woman like you. The Matt I know is a good man who has learned the importance of devotion and consistency the hard way. Your lifestyle indicates that you don't know what devotion or consistency means."

"You can tell all that by appearances, huh?" Samantha's eyes narrowed with dawning belligerence.

"You go out of your way to make that impression obvious. So I'm asking you to leave Matt alone and concentrate on someone else. He's taken."

"He's taken?" Samantha's response grew increasingly tense. "Do you really believe that?"

"Yes, I do. As I said, Matt is a good man. He's faithful to his commitments."

"No matter how they rankle?"

Jenny's color darkened. "They didn't rankle until you showed up."

"But they do now." Not quite understanding her motivation, Samantha took an aggressive forward step. Noting that they were drawing interested glances, she lowered her voice and continued. "If Matt really loved you, he wouldn't have spent last night with me, and this warning wouldn't be needed."

"You're lying! Matt did not spend the night with you!"

Samantha did not reply.

Drawing herself up shakily when Samantha remained silent, Jenny continued. "If he did, you simply took advantage of a weak moment . . . of a masculine need that Matt could not control."

"He made no attempt to control it."

"But he regrets his actions! He despises himself for what he did!"

"I truly doubt that."

Again in control, Jenny said firmly, "I came here to tell you that your time with Matt, whatever future you believe it had, is over. It is done, do you understand?"

When Samantha chose not to reply again, Jenny added, "Matt and I have a firm history behind us that will pave the way for our future together. You have nothing."

"Nothing but passion."

"Passion fades."

"Ours won't."

"You're in for a surprise," Jenny warned.

"No, you are."

Appearing unable to continue the soft-spoken but heated conversation, Jenny said simply, "Stay away from him. In the end, it will be for your own good, as well as for Matt's and mine."

Concluding their conversation abruptly, Jenny turned on her heel and headed for the mercantile, leaving Samantha to face a silent but deadening truth.

She was jealous.

Her emotions confused, Samantha was suddenly determined in spite of all else that she would remain in Winston until she could accomplish her goal. Yet admittedly, her instincts were untrustworthy and her behavior made a mockery of the dedication for which her father gave his life.

She knew of only one answer. His name was Sean McGill.

Before she could change her mind, Samantha walked to the stagecoach office to send a telegram. She emerged a few minutes later, already beginning to regret her actions. Sean would come—she knew he would—yet she should not have wired him. She should have worked out the situation by herself. Calling him in was akin to admitting a defeat, and she had never admitted defeat before.

Samantha became suddenly determined. With any luck, she would prove herself by aggressively searching every inch of Matt's land for physical evidence of his guilt *before* Sean came.

And there was no time to start like the present.

Jenny smiled as she turned off onto the trail, but her smile fell as soon as she was out of sight of town. The midday sun of the pleasant day beat down on her head, but she did not feel its warming rays. Her heart was broken after her encounter with Samantha Rigg.

She had ended their conversation and had entered the mercantile to shop as if nothing unusual had occurred. She had braved the curious gazes and the whispers that had abounded, all the while admitting to herself that she was more shaken than she had imagined she would be.

The revelation that Samantha Rigg was lovely despite the heavy makeup and gaudy dress that displayed her womanly assets clearly had been difficult. Yet despite her outer harshness, the saloon woman had sounded sincere in her feelings for Matt.

The familiar question returned.

"Aren't you tired of running away?"

She had avoided the true meaning behind the phrase that Matt had uttered so many years ago. The true solution to her problem was not to speak to Samantha as she had originally thought. She needed to speak to Matt. She had known him all her life. He would tell her the truth no matter how much it hurt them both.

Resolved, Jenny slapped her wagon's reins against old Stormy's back and clucked the aging gelding to a faster pace. She needed to get home so she might store her groceries and then visit Matt at his ranch. He was amply chaperoned by Willy and Nat, and even if his two hired men should not be present, Pa would not protest. He would believe she simply wanted to see her betrothed. He would—

Jenny's thoughts halted abruptly when Matt

appeared unexpectedly on the road in front of her. Her heart flip-flopped at the sight of him.

Matt rode up beside her with a half smile. "Hello, Jenny. I needed to see you today so we could talk."

"I need to talk to you, too," Jenny responded simply.

"I thought we might ride together to a place where we'll have a little privacy."

"All right."

Jenny's heart pounded as she prepared to step down from her wagon in the privacy of a forested glade a few minutes later. Her breathing shortened the moment Matt touched her hand. She could not help responding to the warmth in his gaze when he then slid his arm around her familiarly and guided her to the sunny spot to sit.

She waited until Matt began hesitantly, "I have something to tell you, Jenny."

"I know already." Upset, attempting to avoid a confession that would stir unpleasant feelings, Jenny turned her head. Tears filled her eyes when Matt gripped her chin to turn her gaze back to him and inquired, "What do you know?"

"I know about Samantha Rigg. I know that you're attracted to her, and that you . . . you slept with her."

"Who told you that?"

"Samantha did."

Matt's expression revealed his surprise. He scrutinized her sorrowful expression for long moments before he said sincerely, "I'm sorry I hurt you, Jenny."

"It's true, then."

"Yes."

Jenny studied Matt's expression. He did not attempt to evade the truth, and his honesty somehow touched her heart. He had not meant to hurt her. But he had.

"Why, Matt?" she replied instinctively. "Didn't you understand what the future we had planned together and the candor that we always expected from each other meant? Didn't you realize that you could come to me no matter how you felt? Didn't you know that I'd try to make things right for you whatever it cost us?" And lastly, "Didn't you comprehend how learning about it all after everyone else would make me feel?"

Jenny waited the long moment until Matt finally responded, "I don't really know why I did it. I only know that I did, and that I regret it at this moment even more than I imagined I could."

The new, indefinable quality in Matt, as well as his deep and true sense of remorse, moved her. Never touched so deeply before, Jenny asked in a whisper, "Was it because Samantha Rigg is beautiful? I mean, I know I'm plain. I've always known I'm plain, just like I always knew you deserved so much more."

"You're not plain, Jenny." Matt was defensive. "Maybe some people might say that at first glance, but it's not true. You're wholesome, that's all, and you've proved that you're real and understanding with everything you just said. I sensed those qualities in you the first moment I saw you. That means much more to me now that I'm older and wiser than being beautiful ever could. Everything I just said is true, just like the fact that you're too good for a man like me is true."

"Does that mean—?"

"If you think I'm trying to find a way to call everything off between us, you're wrong." Matt's response was adamant.

Jenny unconsciously released a relieved breath. "I'm glad." She continued shakily. "Truthfully, I didn't know what I was going to do when I saw you today, but right now I just want to know why. Why did you do it, Matt?"

Matt shook his head. "I wish I could truthfully answer that question." His light eyes shone with a glow she had never witnessed before when he continued. "There are a lot of questions that I wish I could answer right now, but there's one thing I know for sure. What I felt for Samantha was fleeting. What I feel for you is entirely different."

"You're sure?"

"It occurs to me suddenly that in the back of my mind I always wanted someone like you, Jenny— someone I could talk to, someone whose understanding nature proves she really cares about the real me. You're a wish come true."

Touched by his softly spoken words, as well as by an inner quality she was unable to ignore, Jenny did not move as Matt slowly lowered his mouth toward hers. Yet she was unprepared for the wealth of emotion that Matt's gentle kiss generated. She responded when his caresses grew more yearning and his kiss deepened. She trembled with a similar desire when Matt struggled to control his burgeoning emotion.

Their excitement increased with each kiss.

The wonder grew greater with each caress.

Bewildered by the unexpected emotion between them, Jenny drew back from Matt abruptly. Not quite certain of her reasoning, she said breathlessly, "I . . . I have to go home now, Matt."

Matt was unnaturally silent, his gaze unexpectedly dark. She sensed a protest he did not utter as he helped her back onto the wagon seat. Yet she was startled when he stepped up to sit beside her and then took her into his arms to kiss her with unrelieved passion.

Visibly shaken, he then handed her the reins and stepped back onto the ground.

Not sure what to do then, Jenny clicked old Stormy into motion and rode off without daring to look back.

Tucker smarted as he rode toward the cabin hidden in the Texas wilderness of his brother's land. He had known he had to meet Jenny, and he had taken the first opportunity to do so—provided by his encounter with her on the roadway a short time earlier.

She had believed he was Matt.

Tucker's expression grew dark. He had intended to take advantage of her in order to make Matt angry, but the trouble was that Jenny hadn't been what he expected. Oh, she was as plain as people said she was, if a person chose to think of her that way. She was self-demeaning because of it, and that hurt him somehow, but she had proved she had more to offer than physical beauty. The truth was that he had never met a woman like her before, a woman who looked him straight in the eye even though her question was difficult. Yet she had proven understanding beyond belief, especially when he confirmed her suspicions about an affair with Samantha Rigg in Matt's stead. His response had been vague and inadequate, but she had forgiven him because he said he was sorry, and she believed he was.

Strangely enough, he *was* sorry for her obvious pain, even if he wasn't responsible for it.

Tucker was suddenly enraged. Jenny had responded to him passionately despite the straying he had confessed to in his brother's stead, but he was intensely aware that it was not Tucker Conroy, Matt's errant younger brother, who stirred her. It was Matt Strait . . . the *privileged* Matt Strait.

Tucker ran a hand through the sweat-darkened hair underneath his Stetson in a frustrated gesture that he and Matt shared. He took a deep breath, expanding the powerful chest he had clutched Jenny against so briefly. He wondered how it would feel to be loved by a woman like Jenny, whose innate gentleness seemed capable of soothing even the most deeply buried pain. He was aware that had he been less considerate of her recent distress and more insistent during those few moments previously, he could have overwhelmed her.

Yet he had let her get away.

Why?

His cabin came into view and Tucker halted his horse to survey the surroundings. Satisfied that all was clear, he rode up to the dilapidated structure, dismounted, and tied up his mount.

Why?

That question lingered.

Chapter Five

Samantha walked down the stairs of the Sleepy Rest Hotel. It was early—much too early for a young woman who had not gotten to bed until the wee hours to be up and about, but she was counting on that. Grateful that the registration desk was vacant and that the clerk was probably still sleeping, she continued on toward the street with a definite destination in mind.

Samantha stepped out onto the boardwalk, noting that the sun was just beginning to rise and the town itself had barely begun coming to life. That also pleased her. She knew she wouldn't be asked too many questions she couldn't answer truthfully at the early hour, and when she returned, the town would be too busy with comings and goings for anyone to notice her arrival on the crowded street.

Samantha walked quickly. Too much time had passed with nothing accomplished. Matt had not been back to see her since the night they had spent together and since her confrontation with Jenny several days earlier. She was uncertain if Jenny had faced Matt down as well as her, but it made little difference. Matt obviously regretted their time together or he would have returned.

Sean McGill had not yet responded to her wire, either. She was happy about that—she was almost sure. In any case, she was determined that when he came, she would have the proof she had originally come to Winston to get.

She had maintained her masquerade at the Trail's End although evenings had crawled past with deadening slowness. Her original mission was clearer than ever before. Allowing her emotions to cloud her judgment with Matt still smarted, but becoming a Pinkerton detective was a lifelong dream. She would not—*she could not*—allow anything else to take precedence.

With that thought in mind, she had purchased a casual blouse, split skirt, and boots, aware that she would need that attire in order to ride astride while searching Matt's property. She had spent the early morning hours secretly searching it for three days already. If she was as lucky as she hoped to be, she would discover the needed evidence against him somewhere. She suffered for lack of sleep, but she had begun eagerly anticipating morning, when she would ride out like a true Pinkerton in search of the proof she needed.

Gratified to reach Toby's livery without being noticed, Samantha turned abruptly at the sound of Toby's voice.

"Here again, I see."

"Yes, here again." Samantha could not help smiling at the sight of Toby's lined, disapproving expression. He didn't like to see her riding out secretly and alone, but he was always there when she came to get a horse. His constancy struck a warm chord inside her. "Is my mount ready?" she asked.

Toby's gray mustache twitched as he ignored her question and replied casually, "You know I never asked you what you're doing riding out so early in the morning, especially since you don't ever get out of the Trail's End until the wee hours."

"I know."

"I never asked, neither, why you return just in time for your job at the Trail's End, or why you refuse to discuss where you went."

"I know."

"I won't never ask, neither, 'cause it ain't nobody's business, including mine."

"That's right."

Toby mumbled an unintelligible word and then reaffirmed, "I respect your privacy, you know."

Samantha sensed the axe was about to fall when Toby's face suddenly flushed and he continued with considerable heat. "But I'm getting damned tired of seeing them circles under your eyes getting darker every day. I don't know what you're up to, but I figure all this secrecy ain't normal and you're going to get yourself into trouble."

"I don't want to talk about it, Toby. Besides, you said you respect my privacy."

"I do, but I warned you that Matt Strait had previous commitments no matter how close you two seem to get. And I ain't going to stand by while you make yourself sick over something that might still be happening between the two of you."

"You don't have to worry about me, Toby." Samantha swallowed past the lump in her throat brought on by his comments and continued determinedly. "I won't get sick."

"You're well on your way, 'cause you don't get enough sleep."

Deciding to take the offensive, Samantha replied, "How do you know where I'm going or what I'm doing? How do you know I don't go somewhere where I rest most of the day?"

"Them circles under your eyes speak for you," Toby responded. "Not that they ain't becoming in a way. They make you look kind of fragile."

It was Samantha's turn for her nose to twitch as she said, "If there's one thing I'm not, it's fragile." Determined to end the conversation before she said something she regretted, Samantha said quietly, "I'll make you a deal, Toby. I'll take a day off soon, just to satisfy you."

"That won't satisfy me."

"What will satisfy you?"

"I need you to make me a promise."

Samantha's frown deepened. She responded tentatively, "What kind of promise?"

"I want you to promise me that whatever you're doing, you won't do nothing dangerous unless you talk to me first."

Samantha paused. Toby had kept her confidence so far. He didn't ask much. She responded impulsively, "All right, I promise."

"You're sure?"

Samantha paused to scrutinize the thin, graying old fellow with the concerned expression. He really was a dear old man. The least she could do was relieve his fears.

She replied firmly, "Yes."

Quiet, obviously restraining any further questioning, Toby then led her to a gelding that was saddled and waiting. Again surrendering to impulse, she kissed his cheek before mounting and turned to say, "Don't worry about me, Toby. I'll be fine."

Those last words to Toby before riding out of town rang in Samantha's mind as she walked over a vast field littered with gopher holes. The moist heat of afternoon grew more intense, and both she and the limping mount she dragged behind her felt it. She had spoken so confidently to Toby an hour earlier, but she had not anticipated that the morning would turn incredibly hot and humid; that in her rush, she would forget to fill her canteen; that her gelding would throw a shoe and go lame, forcing her to dismount and walk; or that she would get totally lost in an unfamiliar area of Matt's vast holdings.

Samantha cursed her luck as the sun rose higher, as the morning grew hotter, and her shirt stuck to her like a second skin. Perspiration ran down the back of her neck. Her scalp was soaked and her spirits were plummeting. She pushed her hat back irritably. At the present rate, she would not make it back to town in time for her customary appearance at the Trail's End. She knew others might not question her absence, but she was sure Toby would, and any search party he might organize would only call attention to activities she preferred to keep secret.

Still frowning when she came over a rise, Samantha suddenly felt her heart leap. In the distance was a ragged fence that marked a boundary, as well as a fellow working at a break in the line. She scrambled toward the figure, only to halt abruptly when the man slowly straightened and turned to afford her complete recognition.

Damn it all, it was Matt.

Aware that she had no recourse, Samantha continued walking toward him. He reached for his shirt with an expression that did not bode well. She struggled to come up with a feasible excuse for being there, yet the breadth of his bare chest and arms, and the beads of sweat that shimmered on his skin and outlined every contour of his muscular body, distracted her. She remembered only too clearly how eagerly those strong arms had clutched her close against that muscled chest and how sweet the weight of his powerful body had felt when it had lain atop hers. She could not seem to forget it.

The sun continued its relentless assault and Matt frowned more darkly when his shirt adhered to his moist skin, foiling his attempt to cover himself. Having no recourse, he left the faded garment hanging open, unintentionally elevating her awareness of the firm flesh underneath to a breathtaking degree. A trickle of sweat snaked down his chest to disappear into the waistband of his trousers as Samantha forced a smile.

Matt wasn't smiling. He squinted as Samantha drew closer, a limping horse behind her. It occurred to him that he had never seen her without the makeup of a saloon woman. It stunned him that she was even more beautiful. Her gaze appeared an even brighter brown-green when framed by her naturally dark lashes. The planes of her cheeks were shining and colored by the heat of the day. They drew his eyes to her lips, which seemed even more plump and appealing without the heavy gloss of her trade. Her unbound hair was a cascade of color. He longed to touch it.

The fit of her western garb did not please him, however. She had obviously bought her outfit ready-made, and it was too tight. The bulge of her breasts could be clearly seen in the sweat-soaked shirt, and the fit of her split skirt displayed the curve of her backside too obviously to suit him.

Yet he could not seem to stop himself from remembering that the taste of those breasts was sweet beyond compare, and that the curve of her backside had called to him as he had run his mouth along the rounded surface.

Halting his rambling thoughts, Matt cursed silently at the feelings that came to life inside him. He loved Jenny, yet she did not arouse him in any way. But Samantha did . . . endlessly. She excited and challenged him; yet in more intimate moments when other facets of a complex personality emerged, she stirred him to alternating depths of passion and tenderness that shook him to the core. While all else about his feelings for Samantha remained unclear, he could not keep at bay his growing conviction that they had only scratched the surface of emotion between them. He was somehow certain those feelings would take a journey of loving years to explore.

Years.

That simple word brought Matt sharply back to reality as Samantha drew near. A woman like her didn't reckon constancy in *years*.

Aware that his body had reacted spontaneously to the sight of Samantha, Matt attempted to draw his shirt closed. He waited only until she was close enough to hear him before asking darkly, "What are you doing here?"

Appearing unsettled by his manner, Samantha responded, "My . . . my horse threw a shoe. He went lame."

"Why did you come?" he persisted.

"I just went for a ride."

"You're on my property."

"I didn't know where I was," she responded hesitantly. "I guess I got lost."

Matt remained silent, his displeasure apparent.

He didn't believe her.

Samantha stood a few feet from the man who had filled her dreams since the ecstatic night they had spent together. He wasn't pleased to see her, and he was obviously irritated that she was there.

Controlling her angst, Samantha continued to smile while inwardly thinking that it was she who should be angry. Not only had he left her alone in a bed that was still warm from their lovemaking, but she was now dependent on his whims when she had hoped only to redeem her flagging professionalism.

"You got lost, huh? Well, whatever reason you have for coming here, I suppose you can't go back until you have a horse that can carry you."

Samantha raised her chin at Matt's retort. She replied sarcastically, "I don't mean to be a burden."

"You should have thought of that sooner."

Now she understood. Matt wanted no part of her.

Matt secured her mount's lead reluctantly to his

horse. He then swung her up onto his saddle without another word. Before she could react, he had mounted behind her.

Unprepared for the surging emotion that swept all other thought from her mind when Matt's arms closed around her, Samantha went silent. She trembled when he clucked his horse into motion and the heat of his body enclosed hers. His arms were strong, potent in memory. The pressure of his thighs against hers burned. The obvious bulge at his crotch held her breathless as his mount swayed in relentless rhythm. Her objectivity had dissipated completely by the time they reached his ranch house and he said, "Here we are."

Samantha did not respond when Matt dismounted and lifted her down from the saddle. Nor did she react when he held her so close that she slid erotically down the length of his body. She was unable to respond when he hesitated, his mouth only inches from hers, and said darkly, "My hired men brought a small herd to the railhead. They won't be back for a few days."

Silence.

He released her and continued. "I suppose you can wait inside while I shoe your horse."

Samantha started toward the house with Matt's footsteps sounding to her rear.

"The house is empty," Matt repeated as he pushed the door closed behind them. She turned toward him, aware that his breathing was growing heavy and rapid. His light eyes searched hers in the semi-darkness when he suddenly confessed with obvious torment, "You know I didn't want to leave you that morning, don't you?" He did not wait for her to reply as he continued. "I never said I'm sorry, Samantha, but I'll say it now. I'm sorry for what happened. I'm sorry for what can't be. The truth be told, I'm sorry—"

"Don't say you're sorry again." As breathless as he, Samantha could not control the shuddering that racked her as she heard herself whisper, "Please, don't say another word, Matt. Just love me as if there's no tomorrow—and I promise I'll pretend there isn't."

Speechless for long moments, Matt then pulled her hungrily into his arms.

Samantha allowed the invasion of Matt's mouth as they stood just within the doorway of the darkened cabin. The torrid wonder of his kiss deepened, and she did not protest when he loosened her clothing. Leaving her shirt hanging open, he took her breasts into his mouth, seeming as hungry as she for the glory it brought them. She clutched him closer as his ministrations grew fiercer and his appetite for her stronger.

She barely noticed the moment when Matt slipped her split skirt down from her hips and ripped away her small clothes to reveal her naked flesh. The wonder that he induced held her motionless as he caressed her skin with his lips, and trailed his tongue in a taunting downward quest.

Trembling uncontrollably, she was uncertain when he came to the juncture between her thighs. His lips touched the tender slit hidden there, and pure need shot through her. She protested his invasion, only to have him look up at her earnestly and whisper, "However long our loving will last, I want it to be true—all that either of us has ever dreamed it could be. Let me prove it can be that way for us, Samantha."

His gaze was a magic Samantha could not resist. Gradually loosening her grip on Matt's shoulders, she closed her eyes and allowed him to explore the warm delta awaiting him.

She had never felt so alive, so loved, so much a part of a man as Matt's kiss drove deeper into her moistness. Her trembling increased and she clutched him tight with hands that had formerly restrained him—enabling, wanting.

An uncontrollable yearning grew inside her. She gasped at its heat as Matt kissed her more deeply. She groaned and pled with unintelligible words she could not seem to restrain. She twisted and trembled. Her knees weakened and Matt held her upright, cupping her buttocks with hands that afforded support while also providing greater access to his ministrations. She was enthralled by a scope of loving that elevated her to a realm she had never inhabited before.

Her world careened with colliding colors when the first shuddering tremors enveloped her. Surrendering to the overwhelming pleasure, she was transported to a place where only emotion survived.

Samantha's strength weakened when the trembling concluded. Her legs were unable to support her, and she crumpled to her knees. When she opened her eyes again, she was face-to-face with Matt, being held upright by his strong arms as he whispered, "This is only the beginning, Samantha."

Matt scooped her into his arms, leaving her clothing behind as he carried her to a small bedroom and closed the door behind him. He removed his own clothing, aware that she watched as he revealed every inch of male flesh.

Naked at last, hard and ready, he moved to the bed and lay down beside her. He took only a moment to strip away her remaining garments before entering her with a single thrust. Halting at her gasp, he repeated, "This time is ours, Samantha."

Gasping as he slid deeper, as his motions grew more rapid, as she joined him while emotions flew high and wide, Samantha ascended a pinnacle that could be breached in only one way.

Climax came again in a burst of simultaneous glory when Matt's strong body moved convulsively atop hers. She clutched him close when they came to rest at last. Eyes closed, she indulged in the beauty of the moment.

Stirring at an insistent sensation, Samantha

opened her eyes to see Matt staring down at her with a gaze that was hot with longing. She remained silent as he whispered, "There is no one else in the world right now—just the two of us."

Samantha swallowed at the solemnity of his words. She heard herself whisper a single word in response.

"Promise?"

She saw Matt smile briefly before he replied in quiet earnest, "I promise."

Tucker rode slowly into Winston. The main street was buzzing with early afternoon activity, with the comings and goings of wagons as shoppers visited the mercantile to fill their larders, and with towns-folk doing their daily chores before darkness closed in and a night crowd took over with subdued revelry.

The truth was that he liked Winston. He liked the town and he liked being part of the horsemen arriving for the night's revelries when work was finished for the day. He knew his brother wouldn't be one of them, of course. He had studied his brother's routine so they wouldn't both appear in the same place at the same time and compromise his dual identity. He had learned that Matt was too dedicated to the ranch to leave it alone now that his men had taken a herd to the railhead. Matt would remain at his ranch until his men returned.

Tucker had done his best to practice Matt's mannerisms in order to be successful at the deception. Matt's speech was not difficult to imitate since they both had the same deep tone of voice. Their features were so identical that even he wouldn't have been able to tell them apart. To further perpetuate the charade, Tucker's shirt was worn but spotlessly clean, and his trousers fit snugly from constant washings. Tucker had even taken to wearing his hair curling at his collar, since Matt had little time for a barber's skills. There was little difference in the outward appearance of the two men. The only thing he wasn't able to duplicate was the belt buckle that their father had bequeathed to Matt.

Yet like their father, despite the similarities between them, Matt still refused to acknowledge him.

That thought angering him, Tucker became more determined. He would use the dual identity Matt had afforded him to his best advantage until that time. No one would suspect he was an imposter until Matt had had enough.

Tucker laughed. Once Matt openly declared his existence, he intended to go into hiding so Matt needed to *prove* he existed.

Once he was proven to be Matt's twin, he would then claim half the ranch as part of his inheritance—a plan he was certain that Matt did not suspect.

Tucker smiled more broadly. What would Matt do then?

Yes, revenge was sweeter than honey.

"Matt, wait up a minute!"

Tucker drew his mount to a halt and then turned toward the gruff voice to see Toby Larsen motioning him toward the boardwalk. He had done his homework and knew that the old man was an acquaintance of his brother's, although he had been closer to the father than the son. Yet the old fellow appeared intense.

Tucker maintained his smile when he dismounted. The gray-haired fellow said with a worried frown, "Well, you prove me wrong again. I thought I had it figured out what Samantha was doing these past three days, but it looks like I made a mistake—which makes me even more worried than before."

Somehow annoyed, Tucker asked flatly, "What are you talking about, Toby?"

"I'm talking about Samantha Rigg—you know, the new woman at the Trail's End? I don't figure I need to remind you who she is."

"I know who you're talking about."

Toby nodded. "I bet you do."

Tucker pressed, "Say what you wanted to say and get it over with. I have to visit the mercantile and I'm thirsty. The bar is calling me."

"If you're too busy to talk—"

Tucker's light eyes narrowed as he warned, "Just say what you have in mind, old man."

Toby's small eyes scanned his expression irritably. "I can't say I like your tone, but I've got other things in mind right now, especially since it's getting late and Samantha ain't back in town yet."

"So?"

"So she's been leaving town early in the morning and returning in time for work. I figured she was visiting you, but I guess I was wrong."

Tucker was immediately alert. "Leaving town early every day, you say?"

"For the past three days, anyway." Toby shook his head. "To tell you the truth, I'm worried about her because she wouldn't say where she was going. Since it wasn't to your place . . ."

Toby's voice drifted away as Tucker tensed. Samantha had turned him down flat when he came into town and caught her going back to her hotel, but he had no doubt where she was at that moment.

Toby continued. "I stopped all the talk about your dealings with Samantha, Matt, 'cause nobody wants to cross me openly. But she ain't been the same, and I figured she was taking matters into her own hands. I warned her from the beginning that your mind was set on Jenny, and nobody was going to get in your way."

"Jenny . . ."

"But if you don't know nothing about why she's been setting out so early in the morning—"

"Who said I didn't know?"

"You did, damn it!" Toby's small eyes flashed with unexpected temper.

"You had it in your mind that Samantha went out to see me. You didn't give me a chance to explain that I met up with Samantha this morning and she told me she might not be coming back to town tonight because she's been visiting a friend."

"A friend? Samantha's a stranger in town."

"So's her friend." Tucker leaned a little closer. "Her friend used to work with her, but she's married now, and she has two kids that she's finding hard to handle. Samantha is helping her on the sly."

"I don't know about nobody new moving into the area."

Ignoring Toby's response, Tucker continued. "Samantha doesn't want anybody to find out what she's doing. It'll make it hard on her friend, so don't tell anybody . . . and don't go looking for her. She said she'll be back as soon as she's able to."

"Hmmm . . ."

Tucker waited as Toby digested his story. It was weak, but it was the best he could do on short notice.

Tucker felt a slow heat suffusing his senses. The truth was that he knew where Samantha was, all right. He had thought his brother appreciated Jenny for the decent woman that she was, but it appeared he did not.

Tucker knew what he had to do. His attention snapped back to Toby when the old man responded, "If you say so, Matt."

Tucker added gruffly, "I don't think Samantha would want you to go looking for her."

"No, I wouldn't do that. I already told her that I respect her privacy."

"Yeah . . ."

"I'll just wait for Samantha to come back."

But the old man didn't appear to believe his own words.

Unwilling to think any further on it, Tucker tied up his horse and walked into the mercantile. He made a quick purchase, then walked back onto the street and remounted without visiting the saloon.

He knew what he had to do. Matt was lucky. He had been lucky all his life. It was about time his luck came to an end.

There was no past . . . no future, only the present.

Shaking with need, Matt kept that thought in mind as he pressed his mouth against Samantha's sweet flesh. The simple bed on which they lay rocked with the weight of their loving as he explored a trail along Samantha's naked flesh that he had taken before. But the heat between them was hotter when he found the bud of her passion at last. His need was greater as he sucked and licked the moisture from the sweet crevice that he had sought. Her groans were louder and more impassioned as his loving assault deepened. Her body's homage to his loving was more profuse when he drew it again deep within him, savoring the taste.

His emotion heightened as her cries grew more intense, as her body shook and spewed forth another spontaneous offering, as he swallowed again and again, hoping the moment and the taste of her would never end.

But it did.

Samantha was still trembling when Matt slid himself up upon her naked length. He listened to her rasping breaths, aware that they echoed his own, and then turned in a swift movement that found his back flush against the mattress with Samantha's body lying atop his. He closed his eyes, enjoying the sensation of her soft breasts pressed against his chest, of the moisture between her thighs, still warm from his loving.

Aware that their joining had bound them closer than he had believed possible, he kissed Samantha's closed eyelids, ran his lips against the contours of her cheek, and then covered her parted lips with his.

His kiss deepened. His body ached and swelled again. Fitting himself snugly against her, he entered her with a sudden upward thrust.

Samantha's eyes opened wide at his unexpected penetration. Uncertain, she lifted herself atop him and stared down into his face. Her naked breasts teased his lips, and Matt took them to suckle greedily.

Swallowing, circling the roseate tips, consuming them avidly, he was uncertain of the exact moment when Samantha responded to his ministrations—when she opened herself to him and began a heated dance of her own atop his nakedness. He remembered only the moment when, still joined, Samantha drew herself back to toss her unbound hair away from her face, and with eyes closed and arms held high, she met his penetrations with a zest that sent him over the edge of rapture.

He climaxed then, his heated shudders reverberating inside Samantha until she collapsed against him and they lay exhausted and complete in each other's arms.

He did not want Samantha to stir, but she did. Raising her head, she looked down wordlessly at him.

He responded to her unasked question with simple words:

"No past . . . no future . . . only now."

He saw tears fill Samantha's eyes as she whispered, "Agreed."

He crushed her close then and held her tight. He did not want to question his feelings. He wanted only to feel.

Tucker took a narrow, hidden trail. The late afternoon sunlight shone hotly on his worn Stetson as he made his way toward Matt's ranch house. Several days had passed since he had allowed Jenny to leave him after their chaste exchange, which had left him surprisingly shaken. Sleepless nights spent in the abandoned cabin where he had taken up residence had also passed, during which he had pondered why he had let her go when he was certain that with a few more whispered words and intimate coaxing, he would have been able to take her then and there.

He had come to a solemn conclusion during his sleeplessness. The answer was simple. Strangely enough, he had experienced a noble moment—nobility that his brother obviously did not share.

Nobility was new to him. He knew now that there was no room for it in his world. He had made a mistake that he intended to correct. But first he needed to be sure.

Tucker moved carefully through the terrain. He had become comfortable with the lay of the land and intended to arrive at the ranch house surreptitiously.

He dismounted a distance from his brother's ranch house and approached it cautiously. Admittedly, he had been unimpressed with the spread at first. From all appearances, it was slowly deteriorating. The cleared area that extended a distance from the house was not well kept. The barn and corral near the structure, the few simple outbuildings, and the remains of a garden that he supposed had once been alive and thriving, all needed work. The place was obviously suffering from debt and the lack of a woman's hand.

Tucker admitted to finding that thought amusing. His mother would not have dirtied her well-kept hands, and she ignored debt of any kind. Her solution was to merely leave it behind. As a matter of fact, it was a wonder that she had remained at the ranch for any length of time at all.

Tucker's brow furrowed at the sight of the two horses tied up at the rail beside the house. He moved silently to the window and stood stock-still at what he saw inside.

Samantha Rigg and Matt. Samantha's hair was unbound and in disarray. Her clothing, as well as Matt's, had been carelessly donned. They stood near the fireplace looking down at a pan of food on the fire. Samantha turned toward Matt. Matt took her into his arms.

The pan on the fire was forgotten.

So it was true!

Tucker stepped back from the window, seething. He knew passion when he saw it. Yet he was somehow surprised at the confirmation that Matt wasn't really any better than he was.

Somehow he wished it weren't true.

Pausing only a moment, Tucker then walked silently back to his horse. He mounted, uncertain of his emotions when he kicked the animal into movement.

His mother had said one thing and his father another.

His brother spoke one way and acted another.

His own noble moment had been for naught.

Only one thing was sure. Jenny was his for the taking.

* * *

Tucker arrived at Jenny's ranch still angry at the scene he had witnessed in his brother's ranch house. In scouting the land, he had learned where Jenny lived, and he had traveled there with haste.

Jenny's background was no mystery to him. He knew her father was all she had left, and that she kept house and cooked for him, as well as for the three men who worked at the Circle O. He had seen Bart, Lefty, and Mike busily repairing fences on the way, leaving the possibility that Randolph Morgan was working without them somewhere else. If he were lucky—

Refusing to complete that thought, Tucker dismounted and knocked boldly on the door. Jenny responded to his appearance with a spontaneous smile, but his own smile faded when her father walked up behind her and extended his hand.

"I'm glad to see you, Matt." Randolph Morgan's voice was gravelly, but the pride in the old man's eyes despite a curved posture that bespoke his age was apparent as he continued. "Jenny and I have been waiting for you to show up. Been busy, have you?"

"Yes, sir. I've spent more time than I should have at the ranch." Pretense his forte, Tucker continued. "But I hope to make up for my neglect by taking Jenny for a ride this afternoon."

Randolph looked at him curiously. "I admit to surprise that you're taking time off in the middle of a workday."

"I finished what I intended to do, and I wanted some time with Jenny if she's available."

"Of course I have time for you!" Jenny interrupted, turning to her father as she said, "I won't be long, Pa. Everything is ready for supper, but I'll be back before then."

Randolph's smile was wry. "I guess I forgot for a moment how it was to be young."

Tucker felt the old man's eyes follow him as he saddled Jenny's horse and they rode away. Riding along a sunlit trail a short time later, Tucker suggested, "There's a nice glade nearby where we can dismount and talk."

"I know. What I don't know is what's so important to talk about that you had to come to see me in the middle of the day."

Tucker shrugged as he turned his horse into the glade. "Maybe I just missed you."

"I know I missed you."

Tucker looked up as Jenny continued soberly. "But I need to know, is something wrong?"

"Nothing's wrong." Tucker dismounted when they reached the shadowed glade and lifted Jenny down from her horse and said more softly, "Unless wanting to see you is wrong."

Jenny was so close to him that her body touched his as she replied, "You never invented reasons to see me before, Matt. That's one thing that's different. You're not wearing that belt buckle that you've worn every day since your father's death, and that's another." She added, "The third thing is the way you make me feel."

With a sudden need to hear her say the words, Tucker replied, "How do you feel, Jenny?"

"I thought you knew." Jenny's brown eyes worshipped his as she whispered, "I love you, Matt. I've always loved you. When you talked about marriage between us, it was the answer to my prayers. Even though I knew there was no real magic between us, we knew each other so well that I was sure it was right. My only concern was that you're so handsome, and I'm so plain."

"You're not plain."

"I am."

"No, you're not!" Livid, Tucker grasped Jenny's arms tightly and insisted, "I told you, you're wholesome and you're honest. There's a quality in you that makes your brown eyes sparkle and your features shine."

"They shine only for you, Matt."

Tucker winced at her use of Matt's name.

"What's wrong?"

"I don't know." Tucker stepped back and shook his head. He walked toward the nearby stream, aware that their mounts followed and began drinking. He stared at the horses for a long moment, and then turned to look at Jenny as she walked up beside him. He said with more honesty than he had intended, "I think the way I feel about you is new to me."

"It shouldn't be, since we've known each other for such a long time." She shook her head as she admitted, "But the way I feel is new to me, too, somehow."

Tucker stared at Jenny and then asked, "What's different about it?"

"I don't know. I feel a sense of anticipation when I see you that I never felt before." Her face colored as she proceeded determinedly, "And the way I feel when you kiss me. It's like . . . like you feel the same thing I feel . . . hungry, maybe."

"Hungry . . ."

"For more than food."

Tucker stared harder. He had never met anyone like Jenny before. She spoke to him so openly, declaring her emotions without shame. He felt as if he were drowning in the warm depths of her eyes. They touched a part of him he hadn't known existed.

"Kiss me, Matt."

"Jenny . . ."

"I want to know if I dreamed the way I felt, or if it's really true."

"Jenny, I came here to—"

Lifting herself on tiptoe, Jenny slid her arms around his neck and pressed her mouth against his. Her chaste kiss more than he could bear, Tucker grasped Jenny tight against him. He pressed his mouth deeper, clutched her closer, strained her against him until her slender body melded to his and their kiss left them breathlessly wanting more.

Tucker groaned as he drew back from her. He had never felt this way with a woman before. Jenny wiped away the past, cleansed him of all wrong-doings, made him feel new and unlike the man he had once been.

"I love you, Matt."

Tucker returned sharply to reality.

"I'm waiting to hear you say you love me, too."

Tucker stared down at Jenny . . . sweet, loving Jenny who had no idea that she was in the arms of an imposter. She didn't deserve that.

"Matt . . ."

"I have to go now, Jenny."

"Go?"

Tucker pushed Jenny away firmly. "I . . . I have something important to take care of."

"Did I say something wrong?" Jenny's expression grew pained.

"No, this has nothing to do with you."

"I don't know what you mean, Matt."

"I have to go."

Tucker lifted her back onto the saddle of her nearby horse, ignoring her protests when he mounted as well. He turned out of the glade and back onto the trail, aware that Jenny followed behind. The tears in her eyes cut him deeply when she drew up alongside and whispered, "Tell me what I did, Matt."

Tucker did not respond. He still had not replied to her question when he delivered Jenny to her

ranch and turned his horse back onto the trail with
her earnest pleas echoing behind him.

Toby wandered through his livery stable nervously.
Unable to remain still, his concern deepening, he
looked again at the sky, where a setting sun forecast
the end of another day. Samantha still had not returned from her daily trek. He had not inquired
what she was looking for or what she intended when
she left that morning. He had learned early on that
Samantha had her own mind, and that his affection
for her did not allow him to question her.

He trusted her. He knew that whatever she was
about, she had good reason for it.

And Matt had explained where she was. Yet . . .

Toby walked out onto the busy Winston street.
The Trail's End was alive with color; it would be another lively night. The regulars would miss Samantha there if she did not return. *He* would miss her.
Although she appeared to be a saloon woman like
the others, Samantha was different in a way that
had nothing to do with her natural beauty. He had
known that from the first day, even if he could not
put into words exactly what he sensed.

Admittedly, Samantha had become the daughter
he had lost in another lifetime far away from this
place. She stirred memories he had once chosen to
forget, but they were cherished memories, just as he
cherished Samantha. What concerned him now was

that he could not escape the feeling that something had happened.

"Don't worry about me. I'm fine. I'll see you soon."

An unexpected thickness filled Toby's throat when he recalled Samantha's words. She didn't want him to suffer needlessly. He appreciated that thoughtfulness.

He could only hope that Matt had told him the truth and that Samantha was not at his ranch, waiting for him to return as he secretly suspected. He had seen the way they looked at each other, and he knew Matt's previous commitments. He had the feeling that the dear girl was in for more trouble than she imagined.

He had seen the determined look in Samantha's eyes. She would return when she was good and ready. For the time being, he needed to wait.

The sky outside the ranch house darkened as Samantha stirred. She felt the warmth of Matt's arms around her, and she smiled. It wasn't like last time, when she had awakened alone.

Samantha kept her eyes closed as a wave of uncertainty swept her. She hadn't truly intended to find herself in Matt's bed when she started out that morning. She wasn't sure exactly how or why she was there, except she had been unable to resist the look in Matt's eyes that said so clearly that he wanted her as much as she wanted him.

She did not comprehend her feelings the evening

when he behaved so obnoxiously and she had felt actually repelled by him. She could only conclude that it was an aberration, since in his bed with his arms wrapped around her and with his loving words in her ears, she loved him.

Matt had not said those words. Perhaps he never would. She sensed that something remained between them.

Of course, it was Jenny.

Suddenly uncertain, Samantha started. Or perhaps it was all a dream.

"What's the matter?"

The light-eyed gaze that came into her line of vision when she opened her eyes was familiar. The mouth that briefly covered hers, forestalling a reply, was equally familiar. Still groggy from awakening, she became aware that she was naked underneath the light coverlet and that Matt was as naked as she. Samantha flushed.

"I'm hungry."

"So am I."

Matt kissed her again. His kiss sought to intensify when Samantha drew back unexpectedly and said, "I'm hungry for food."

"You said that before. I hope you realize we'll have to scour that burned frying pan."

Samantha chided, "You don't sound disappointed that it burned."

"I guess I'm not." Matt kissed her again. He threw back the coverlet and stood, unashamedly naked.

"But I guess I'm hungry for food, too. Let's see what I have in the cupboard."

An hour later they had consumed smoked ham, dried and reconstituted vegetables, coffee, and biscuits. They had also conversed and laughed, yet a familiar hunger remained.

They were tight in each other's arms later when Samantha looked out the window at the slowly rising moon.

"I guess I'm going to be staying here tonight."

"I guess you are," Matt mumbled in response.

Samantha surprised herself by asking, "Do you have any regrets?"

"Do I look like I do?"

Matt clutched her close then, and Samantha abandoned herself to his arms and the wonder they raised.

It was only later, in the darkness of the night, that Samantha realized Matt had not really answered her.

And she wondered.

Chapter Six

He was hiding something.

"I don't have time to talk." Matt's reply to Samantha's casual question became surprisingly cautious after they finished breakfast at the start of the new day. Still standing beside the table where they had eaten, he looked at her in a way totally unlike the man who had just shared a pleasant meal with her, and who had made torrid love to her the previous night. He added, "I have to feed the animals."

She supposed that meant no more questions.

Samantha glanced at the sun shining through the windows of the ranch house as he walked out into the yard. The sunbeams lighting the house's interior did not match Matt's sudden mood.

Samantha scrubbed a little harder at the same frying pan they had thoughtlessly burned the evening before, and her heart thumped responsively despite her fatigue. Truthfully, Samantha had not realized how deep her reactions to Matt could be, or that she could expend that much energy in his arms. Yet her sleeplessness had been worthwhile.

They had arisen that morning and had eaten a leisurely, intimate breakfast—eggs from Matt's chickens in the rear coop and bacon cured in Matt's own smokehouse, accompanied by the strong, hot coffee that Matt insisted upon. She had even made biscuits from a recipe she had committed to memory.

Matt had told her that his father and he had often awakened at dawn and gathered part of their breakfast from the coops in the rear of the house before the sun had risen. Samantha had smiled at the thought, but her smile faded when she recalled that Matt appeared to have regretted telling her even that smallest detail about his past life.

She had waited for him to ask about hers. She had previously only offered disconnected information. She had finally concocted a plausible story that she hoped would satisfy him.

He hadn't asked.

Samantha scrubbed harder, aware that Matt had gathered the dirty dishes automatically after they had eaten, obviously from long practice. He would have done the cleanup, too, but she had offered and he had accepted.

Her nose twitched as she continued to scrub. She'd never do that again.

Matt had appeared to be annoyed that the lock on the door was sticking, but she wasn't surprised. Despite Matt's most diligent efforts, the ranch house had begun deteriorating. It was clean, but the bedroom, the only one, bore the marks of totally male habitation from the ragged coverlet on the bed that only a man could bear, to the curtainless windows that allowed in the sun as soon as it rose, and finally to the uncovered, wooden plank floors.

A woman would have managed a rug of some sort. She would also have replaced the chipped plates and worn utensils in the kitchen, even if she needed to do it slowly, so as not to strain a weary budget.

Then there was the worn settee in the living room that bore the marks of years, and haphazard furniture that was comfortable, but unappealing to a woman's eye. It was obvious that a woman had not lived in Matt's quarters for years.

That thought afforded Samantha unexpected relief, but relief was only temporary. She wondered what changes Jenny would make after she and Matt were married.

Jenny in Matt's bed . . . Matt loving Jenny the way he had loved her . . .

Samantha stiffened; the thought rankled. She had asked Matt to love her, and he had done so, so thoroughly and completely that her heart again thundered in recollection. She had not asked him for more than that . . . and he had not offered.

Samantha forced a shrug, but her introspection stung. She needed to remember that this time with Matt was merely a respite and that Matt had done nothing to disprove anything that the Pinkertons had established previously as fact. Actually, he became silent and morose when she asked him even the simplest question. She could explain his behavior in only one way. He was afraid he would let something slip that he would regret later.

Although their lovemaking was uninhibited, their conversation was not. Yet Matt had been so giving and loving when he had held her in his arms that she could not imagine he was the thief she had hoped to bring to justice.

She was so conflicted.

Samantha listened to the sound of Matt's footsteps as he walked toward the barn. She struggled to believe that his commitment to the heritage his father had provided was in too sharp a contrast with criminal acts, yet she knew he was concealing something—something important.

Samantha walked to the window to watch as Matt disappeared into the barn. He would be there tending to the animals for some time. She wanted—she *needed*—to follow through with her investigation. She wanted to be wrong about everything she knew so far to be true about him. She needed to discover that she was chasing the wrong man.

Waiting only a moment longer, Samantha put the frying pan back on the shelf and quickly dried her hands. She then started searching.

She was hiding something.

That thought continued to haunt Matt as he

mucked out the barn. He had already tended to Samantha's horse. A new shoe had done the trick. All that was left to do was to finish up.

Questions filled Matt's mind as he turned to his mount and mumbled, "How do I tell Jenny about Samantha and me? I need to be honest with her. Do I tell her she deserves a man who loves her with passion, not a man who admires her solely for the honest, trusting, and loving person that she is? Is loving her like a brother enough?

"Then how do I tell Samantha after making love to her that there can never be a future for the two of us together? Because that's true, too."

Thunder's ears twitched. Matt's mount turned to look at him curiously, his dark eyes questioning, and Matt was bitterly amused. Now he was talking to a horse. He supposed that would be the only reprieve left to him when Jenny turned her back on him and Samantha did the same.

The truth was that Samantha was everything he had always been wary of in a woman. She was too beautiful, too passionate, and too smart for her own good—like his mother. Like his father before him, he was entranced by her. And like his father before him, he felt he could trust her completely only when she was lying in his arms.

Matt's frustration expanded. He supposed his only alternative was to be totally honest with Samantha about the way he felt—about his burgeoning distrust.

Matt took a deep breath. He supposed there was no time like the present.

Making that sudden decision, Matt propped his rake against the side of the barn and started back toward the ranch house. It did not occur to him that he had approached the house silently, or that he had opened the door quietly, too—until he walked in on the sight of Samantha rummaging frantically through his desk.

Stunned, Matt demanded, "What are you looking for, Samantha?"

Samantha turned toward him guiltily. Obviously taken aback, she stammered before managing, "I was looking for some paper. I wanted to send a note to the bartender at the Trail's End explaining that I'd be back to work tomorrow at the latest."

"How did you expect to deliver your note?"

"I . . . I guess I didn't think that far."

"No, I don't suppose you did." The lines of Matt's face tightened as he demanded softly, "I need to know the truth, Samantha. Why were you searching my desk? What did you expect to find? Money, maybe, or something valuable that would make the night we spent together profitable?"

Samantha gasped.

"Tell me the truth."

The truth . . . she couldn't.

Matt stood silently as Samantha remained motionless. He repeated, "I need to hear the truth, Samantha."

Speaking abruptly from the heart, Samantha replied, "The truth is that the night we spent together was more than I ever dreamed it could be. It was so wonderful that I didn't truly believe it could happen again—and then I realized it probably wouldn't. The truth is that you're betrothed to someone else that you love in a way you don't love me, and that I refuse to be the woman on the side for any man—even you. The truth is that we don't really have a future together, and that truth is more than I can bear."

Matt paled.

Samantha managed a shaky smile as she whispered more softly, "I think I should go back to town now. You did shoe my horse, didn't you?"

Matt nodded.

Samantha glanced at the chair where she had thrown her hat. Grateful that she was otherwise dressed, she felt her smile wobble as she reached for it and said, "I suppose there's nothing left to say."

Matt grasped her arm before she took two steps toward the door. He whispered unexpectedly, "Don't go."

"I must."

"I'm sorry."

"I asked you not to apologize to me again."

Matt gripped Samantha's arms more tightly. "Everything you said about me is true. I am betrothed to another woman . . . a wonderful other woman who I don't want to hurt."

Samantha began trembling. She had known this was coming. She had been warned.

"But now faced with your leaving, I realize I don't want to let you go, either." He swallowed tightly. "I'm going to tell Jenny about us as soon as possible."

"No . . . I mean yes . . . I mean—" Samantha shook her head. "I don't know what I mean."

Matt drew her closer. His lips only inches from hers, he whispered intently, "There's another truth that you didn't mention—the truth that none of this really matters. It only matters what we feel. What do you feel, Samantha?" Matt's light eyes mesmerized her as he asked softly, "Do you want me the same way I want you, with a driving desperation that makes you forget everything else? Do you want me to make love to you until the rest of the world becomes a shadow and the moment is all that's important? Because that's what I want."

Samantha stared at Matt, her throat too thick to immediately respond. Yes, she loved him. Yes, she wanted him. Yes, she needed him. Yes, she wanted all the things he wanted, no matter the cost, although the cost was turning out to be heavier than she had ever imagined it could be.

But then, she had silently answered all his questions beyond doubt.

In the absence of a response she could not utter, Samantha slid her arms around Matt's neck and pressed her mouth to his. Her need deepened when he returned her kiss, returned her caresses, and then drew her tight against him before carrying her to his bed.

The loving took over—a thoughtless, driving, passionate love.

"What were you looking for?"

The unanswered question took on a new significance.

Beams of the noon sun glowed through the windows as Samantha moved around the kitchen, still wrapped in Matt's love. Silent, she felt the afterglow of their lovemaking envelop her, and she knew it affected Matt as well. She saw it in the way he glanced at her surreptitiously, as if to reassure himself that she was there. She felt it in the way his brief glances adored her, just as she adored him, and in the way he turned to her again and again, drawing her close as if the thought of being separated from her was unbearable.

She knew, because she felt the same way. The wonder of him was fresh in her senses, and she—

Samantha gasped aloud when the ranch house door snapped open abruptly to reveal a man standing in the doorway—a man so similar to Matt in appearance that she could see no physical differences between them!

Samantha went rigid with disbelief as she glanced between them. The same dark hair and light eyes, the same severely handsome features and full lips, the same powerful body that Samantha remembered only too clearly lying atop hers.

She gasped again.

Matt's double said heatedly, "So she's still here, you bastard!"

The stranger's harsh tones were so similar to Matt's that Samantha's arms fell limply to her sides. Stepping back from Matt, she could do no more than stare. She was unable to speak when Matt responded, "Yes, I'm a bastard . . . just like you are."

Samantha's eyes widened farther when the other Matt laughed harshly with a smile that she had believed was Matt's own and replied, "Somehow that admission doesn't give me the satisfaction that I thought it would." His expression hardened. "But I want you to know you're responsible for the only two noble moments I've ever had in my life, and that I see now they were both mistakes. Thanks for setting me straight, brother, and for proving to me beyond a shadow of a doubt that I was right all along. You *are* no better than I am."

He turned abruptly and walked back out through the doorway through which he had entered only a few minutes previously.

Twins!

Stunned, Samantha mumbled incredulously, "So that's how he robbed those banks and got away with it."

Realizing abruptly that it was too late to take back those words, Samantha looked at Matt to see his eyes widen. He spoke in a tone of dawning realization.

"So you know my secret. It was my brother who no one knew existed that robbed them, while I was an easy alibi. Are you ready to tell me your secret now, Samantha? Why were you looking through my desk? What did you expect to find—something that explained my part in the bank robberies, maybe?"

"Maybe."

"Who are you? What do you want?"

"You know what I want."

"No, I don't."

Samantha said defensively, "You had your secret and I had mine, but now I understand how you and your brother were able to get away with everything."

Not bothering to confirm or deny her statement, Matt said flatly, "So it's time for you to tell me what you're hiding."

Samantha hesitated, and then said, "I'm not what you thought I was. I'm not a dance hall girl."

"That's not really news to me."

"I came here looking for you . . . hoping to get evidence about the bank robberies that other detectives had failed to get."

"Why? Was it for the reward?"

"Money had nothing to do with it!"

"What was your reason, then?"

"I wanted to prove I could work efficiently as a Pinkerton detective despite my sex."

"A Pinkerton detective?" Matt was incredulous.

"You wouldn't understand."

"Maybe I wouldn't." Matt took a backward step. "Or maybe I just wouldn't care. I thought I knew who you were and how you felt, but it looks to me now that everything between us was just a calculated act on your part. I suppose you'd go to any length to get what you came for."

"That's not true, Matt."

"Maybe it is, and maybe it isn't. All I know for sure is that you lied to me from the first word, and that I couldn't resist you. I was willing to sacrifice my brother's trust and the love of a good woman because of you."

"Matt, listen—"

"No, I'm done listening. It's time for me to act."

"What do you mean?"

"Just get out of here." Grim lines twisted Matt's handsome face into an unrecognizable mask. "You got what you came for. You can tell Pinkerton that you solved a mystery that his other detectives couldn't."

"None of this really makes sense to me, Matt. I need—"

"You have all the information you're going to get from me. The rest is up to you."

"But I don't want to—" Aware that she was about to say she didn't want to leave him, Samantha realized she wasn't sure that was true. How deep was Matt's involvement in the scheme, and why did he protect a brother who obviously hated him?

"You said 'I don't want to'—do what? Leave?" Matt's question was harsh. "That's what you were going to say, isn't it? But the truth is that you want to know why no one seemed to realize I had a twin. I can only assume that's the next question on your mind since you've been trying to get me to talk about myself from day one. Well, that mystery is clear now. It wasn't me you were really interested in."

"Not at first, I wasn't."

Matt's lips clamped tight at her honest response. He then replied more softly, "Go. Your horse is saddled and waiting."

"It's already saddled?"

"I thought you might like to take a ride with me." Matt laughed, his harsh tone matching his brother's and inadvertently sounding so much like him that Samantha took a step back.

"Go! Get out of here!"

Samantha responded to Matt's emphatic commands with a rise of her chin. He had told her to leave. He was a criminal, after all, wasn't he? And she would see to it that justice prevailed.

Samantha did not stop to look back when she mounted her horse and rode out without seeing Matt watching her from the doorway.

Standing in the doorway of the ranch house as Samantha's horse disappeared down the trail, Matt felt numb. The truth was out at last, but he was dead inside. Samantha's covert glances at him in the

Trail's End and the interest that she appeared unable to deny from the start had all been a calculated lie. She had merely carried out a callous strategy worthy of a professional. In doing so, she had proved herself in more ways than one.

Matt walked back into the house and slammed the door behind him. Had she executed similar strategies before in order to prove her worthiness to Pinkerton? Had she responded to other men the same way she had responded to him?

No, she couldn't have!

But then, he wasn't sure.

In the semidarkness of the cabin, Matt faced another admission as well. He had allowed Samantha to use him because he had wanted her. Yet it was now Tucker who would suffer for his weakness.

Confused, Matt was aware of only one thing. Whatever his brother's schemes, he needed to warn Tucker of the imminent danger he faced.

Matt mounted his horse moments later. His mount was winded when he finally arrived a distance from the abandoned cabin his brother had been inhabiting. He dismounted and approached the dilapidated structure carefully. Uncertain of his reception, he drew his gun, hoping it would give him time to explain everything to Tucker. He owed him that much.

He could not fully explain away his own behavior, of course, or the fact that he had ultimately betrayed the woman who was his betrothed and his friend. All he could do was warn Tucker, and prove to him that he was right by admitting that despite their disparate upbringings and the different paths they had chosen, there was really no difference between them.

Taking a breath, Matt burst into the cabin.

It was vacant.

It was obvious that Tucker had not left the area, because most of his belongings were still there. So where was he?

Uncertain, Matt took a moment to decide what to do.

With a sigh, he then sat down to wait.

Riding at full speed, Tucker did not truly realize where he was headed until the Circle O ranch house came into view. Suddenly aware, he drew his mount back to a walk. He had to think, not react. He had to find a way to tell Jenny the truth about his impersonation and that his brother was not really the person she believed him to be because he had betrayed her with another woman.

Strangely, he felt no delight in his mission. Matt was the *good* brother, the *trustworthy* brother, the *hardworking* brother, the brother who was better in every way. Tucker realized that some obscure part of him had wanted that to be true.

But Matt wasn't worthy of Jenny—and neither was he.

Tucker's handsome features creased in a frown.

Strangely, he had never thought of himself as unworthy before. He had merely taken the path of least resistance in order to help support himself and a mother who was too far into drink and other vices to appreciate his effort.

He had never met a woman as straightforward as Jenny before. In truth, he had not truly believed a woman like her existed. It occurred to him belatedly that his life might have been different if he had met her sooner, but it was too late for that kind of thinking.

The truth was that he didn't even think about having sex with Jenny when he talked to her.

Tucker corrected himself. He didn't think *only* about having sex with her, because other facets of her personality continued to amaze him. But he did want her. He wanted to possess her so completely that he could take her goodness inside him. He wanted it to become a part of him.

He wanted so much more.

But Jenny loved Matt.

His mount had come to a halt when Tucker realized that there was only one solution to the problems facing him. He needed to confess everything about his dual identity to Jenny before she learned about it from someone else. He needed to tell her the truth while looking into those brown eyes that seemed to see down into his soul.

Tucker spurred his mount into motion with that

thought in mind. Within minutes he was approaching the Circle O ranch house.

Jenny heard the hoofbeats before she saw the rider approaching. Her father was not home, but she expected him any minute and she walked to the window. Her heart leaped when she saw the rider was Matt.

Dear Matt, loving Matt.

Jenny took a breath and tried to calm herself. The emotion she experienced when Matt approached was new to her. The breathlessness, the anticipation, the realization that he would soon hold her in his arms and touch his lips to hers was almost unbearable.

Suddenly aware of her appearance, Jenny raced to the mottled mirror and attempted to tuck her mousy-brown strands of hair back into the tight bun she wore. She then paused to scrutinize her ordinary features. Brown eyes, brown hair, a lackluster face . . . she was so plain and Matt was so perfect. Matt had said he didn't see her that way. She believed he had meant every word because she had seen honesty in his gaze so clearly that it could not be disputed. Yet the mirror reflection staring back at her challenged that thought.

The hoofbeats drew closer, and Jenny ripped off her apron, smoothed her faded gray calico dress, and raced to the doorway. She was smiling broadly in welcome when Matt dismounted and started toward her. Her smile faded when she saw his sober expression. She knew instinctively that he had come to tell her something, and she feared what it was.

Matt said without preamble, "Is your father home, Jenny?"

"No, he isn't, but he should be home any minute." She said hopefully, "Did you come to see him?"

"No, I came to see you, but I need a few minutes of privacy. I have . . . have something to say."

Jenny's hopes fell. That sober expression was meant for her.

"I'll saddle your horse so we can ride out and be alone for a few minutes."

Jenny's spirits continued to sink as Matt led her saddled mount back toward the house a few minutes later.

Riding astride despite her attire, Jenny did not look at Matt until he motioned her into a familiar glade and lifted her down from her horse. She was not aware that her cheeks were wet with tears until Matt asked, "Why are you crying, Jenny?"

He did not release her as he waited for her to respond.

"Am I crying?" Embarrassed, Jenny attempted to wipe her face dry with her hand. "I hadn't realized . . . I mean . . ."

Suddenly sighing, Jenny looked up at him and whispered, "I've been expecting this to happen. I knew the way I felt when you took me into your arms couldn't last because I knew a man like you couldn't feel the same as I do—not about me."

Matt shook his head. He didn't speak and Jenny rambled, "I had given up on the feelings I was supposed to experience when you kissed me. I figured I would go on for the rest of my life respecting you and loving the goodness in you without feeling true passion. But I suddenly felt alive in your arms in a way I never expected to feel. I felt a new excitement, a new hunger and need."

He was about to speak when Jenny pressed her hand lightly against his lips. "No, don't say anything. I promised that I'd always be honest with you and I needed to say these things. But you don't have to say you feel the same way. The trouble is that I told myself you did. I told myself that your reaction to those moments was more compelling than it ever had been, too. I convinced myself that we had reached the point at last where we not only loved each other, but we desired each other as well."

He drew her closer and he whispered, "Jenny, please, I have to explain—"

"No, don't say anything else. I understand. You've found someone else."

"No!"

"But you came here to speak to me privately. That could mean only one thing."

He shook his head. "It doesn't mean what you think. I didn't come here to deny the way I feel about you. You're like a breath of fresh air to me, Jenny.

You make me complete somehow. You make me feel like a whole person, not the empty, selfish person I've been all my life."

"You haven't been selfish!"

"Yes, I have, in so many ways. But I don't want to see you hurt. Not you, Jenny. I don't ever want to see the light go out of your eyes."

"I told you, Matt, that light is only for you."

He paused to say hoarsely, "Only for me, Jenny?"

"Only for you."

Jenny was not aware that her tears had begun falling again until he brushed them away and said, "Do you mean it, Jenny?"

"I never say what I don't mean."

His lips moved to cover hers, and he kissed her with true hunger.

She could not be certain what happened then. She did not recall when he separated the bodice of her dress and covered her virgin flesh with his mouth. She only knew it was right and good as she clutched him closer.

She was unsure exactly when he stripped away the fragments of her light chemise and slipped her dress down to her ankles with a driving need that rebounded inside her.

Lost in a world of scalding sensation, driven by a voracious hunger, Jenny did not remember the moment when she first felt the ground underneath her back or his muscular body warming hers.

Clutching him closer as myriad sensations winged

through her, Jenny caught her breath when he entered her at last.

Reacting, he questioned tensely, "Did I hurt you?"

She whispered in return, "The pleasure is worth the pain." Then she added, "I love you, Matt."

Strangely, he frowned. Remaining still for long moments, he whispered, "I'll make this all right again for you, Jenny. I promise."

Then sinking himself deeper inside her, he groaned and began plunging again and again in a dance that raised her heart to pounding.

Jenny felt the moment coming. She panicked. Her eyes wide, she whispered, "Matt . . . please . . ."

"I promise . . . to please you as I please myself . . . to love you more than you've ever been loved before . . . to make this a memory that will last a lifetime."

"Make it last?"

But Jenny's gasping words were lost in the spiraling vortex of emotions he brought to life when he plunged one last time and brought them to shuddering fulfillment.

Still in his arms when they were motionless at last, Jenny was stunned at the strength of his grip when he whispered, "I have to tell you something, Jenny. Listen to me until I'm finished, please. Don't be angry." He pleaded again, "Please, don't be angry."

Suddenly trembling, Jenny waited for him to speak.

Chapter Seven

Samantha rode toward town. Matt had run her off. He had acted as if she were his enemy and that since she had finally discovered how the bank robberies had been committed, she intended to take advantage of the information no matter how she felt.

But how did she feel?

That question foremost, Samantha drew back on the reins and slowed her mount's pace. Humidity caused sweat to bead on her skin. Her blouse stuck to her breasts and she pulled the material away from her body, remembering how Matt had loved her so thoroughly that he had—

Samantha refused to finish that thought. Winston was too close, and she wasn't thinking clearly yet. She needed a plan. She needed to remember that Matt now knew the truth about her wanting to become a Pinkerton and her need to prove herself.

But she knew his secret now, too. She wondered

why she hadn't thought about the possibility of twins before.

The unexpected appearance of a familiar figure on the trail ahead of her slowed Samantha to a full stop. She studied the way the rider spurred his horse to a gallop at the sight of her, and the look on his aging face when he slid to a halt beside her.

An inexplicable fear took hold.

Breathless, Toby blurted, "Sean McGill is in town!"

The knot in Samantha's stomach tightened. She had forgotten about Sean.

Toby continued. "When I saw him and he asked about you, I knew I was right in everything I suspected. You sent for him, didn't you?"

Fixed in her masquerade, Samantha responded, "I don't know what you're talking about, Toby."

The downward lines of Toby's face changed when he continued more softly. "I knew from the start that you weren't what you pretended to be, darlin'. I wasn't sure why you had come to Winston, but when I saw your interest in Matt, I had my suspicions."

"Toby, I—"

"Don't get me wrong, I knew what you were feelin' was true. I ain't so old that I don't recognize the kind of emotion Matt brought to life in you, but that's beside the point. I figured you'd get discouraged because I knew Matt was engaged to Jenny and I knew him to be an honest fella. The only thing I didn't count on was that his feelings for you would be so strong."

"Toby—"

"That's where you were right now, right? At Matt's ranch?"

Samantha did not deny it.

He continued. "No matter what happened, I know Matt's feelings for Jenny are deep. Yet I made a mistake in my calculations and now Matt is in trouble."

"Trouble?"

"You know the truth about the robberies, don't you?"

Samantha went momentarily still. She knew what the answer would be when she then asked in a whisper, "You knew about it all along?"

"That Matt has a twin? Yeah, I did."

"But how . . . why?"

"I've been around a long time, Samantha. A real long time. I was Jeremy Strait's friend. I know the whole story about how things were between Matt's mother and him. And I was around when she finally ran off."

"You knew about the twin boys and nobody else did?"

"Flo delivered them at Jeremy's ranch. She didn't need no doctor. At least, she said she didn't. Old Doc Stone is dead anyways, so he can't do no talking. Flo quit the saloon and stayed at the ranch while she was pregnant. She told Jeremy she would marry him as soon as the baby was born. I guess he didn't want to believe she would take off as soon as she got back on her feet, and I don't think he expected that she would take one of the babies with her, either. Anyways, she never came back and everybody just thought Matt was the only baby she had. After Flo disappeared, Jeremy raised Matt and seemed to forget all about Flo. I know everybody else did."

"But Matt had to suspect something."

"Jeremy told him the truth about his mother, that she was a saloon woman and that they were never married. He just didn't mention another baby, that's all. I guess he didn't expect Matt to understand at first, and then when Flo never came back and he never heard about her or his other son again, I guess he figured they were both dead. He was too busy trying to raise Matt and keep his ranch going at the same time, anyways."

Toby continued. "To be truthful, Jeremy was young and hardheaded. I think he wanted Flo to come back of her own accord. As a matter of fact, I think he held out hope that she *would* return someday. But everybody knew Flo was a heavy drinker and that she had every vice in the book. I could never understand what Jeremy saw in her in the first place, or why he wanted her back."

"There must've been something."

"Yeah." Toby wiggled his thick eyebrows expressively. "I figure I know what it was."

"But when you heard about the robberies and the

law came sniffing around after Matt, you didn't mention the twins."

"It didn't occur to me at first. I left the area and started another life after this all came about. I only came back when everything fell apart for me and I had nowheres else to go. Like I said, I forgot about Flo and the other baby. When I did start to suspect the truth, I was the only fella left in town who seemed to know a twin existed. There wasn't no official record of the births because Flo wanted it that way. I wasn't going to tell Matt, so I just kept my mouth shut. I did the same when Sean McGill came around asking questions."

"Sean is—"

"He's a Pinkerton. I remembered him right off, even though he didn't know I did." He shrugged. "Nobody else realized who he was, but everything started making sense to me then. I figured you sent for him and that you're a Pinkerton, too, just like McGill."

"No, I'm not." Samantha saw surprise register in Toby's eyes before she added, "I wanted to be a Pinkerton operative, but Allan Pinkerton didn't want any part of my employment with the agency. I figured getting evidence on the bank robberies was the best way to prove I was worthy of the job."

"What about McGill?"

"My pa was a Pinkerton. Sean McGill was his closest friend and I saw as much of him as I did my father when I was growing up. In the time since Pa's death, Sean has been a kind of surrogate father to me. When I was desperate because everything in Winston was getting out of control, I sent Sean a telegram. Yet I regretted sending it almost the moment it went out. I knew he would come as soon as he could, but I hoped it wouldn't get to him before I could decide what to do."

"What to do about Matt, you mean."

"Right. Never in a million years did I expect that Matt had a twin brother—especially somebody like Tucker, who hates him so much."

"If Tucker hates Matt, I figure it's because Matt is everything that Tucker wishes he was."

"There has to be more to it," Samantha mumbled.

Ignoring her response, Toby asked, "So, now that you know the answer to the mystery, what are you going to do about it?"

Tears filled Samantha's eyes, but she blinked them back as she whispered, "I don't know."

"You'd better make up your mind," he warned. "Sean McGill's got blood in his eye. I figure somebody's going to suffer for it."

"That's my fault." Samantha took a breath. "It's all my fault, but I don't know how to fix it."

"You'd better think up something if you don't intend telling McGill about Tucker."

Toby waited until Samantha said uncertainly, "I don't want to tell Sean anything . . . yet."

"Then you'd better think up something real fast." Looking at the trail ahead, Toby continued in a whisper. "Because here comes McGill right now."

Samantha paled at the sight of the tall, well built older man who came riding toward them with a frown. She could not help the feeling of nostalgia that swept her at the sight of him. She remembered how close her father and he had been, not only in age but in spirit. She remembered that her father had asked Sean to promise that he would look after Samantha for him when he was gone. She knew that under the well-worn worn Stetson that had become Sean's trademark was thick white hair, a face that although lined was as tight and strong as it had ever been, and incredibly blue eyes that revealed he had taken his promise seriously. His promise was exactly what she feared when she gave last minute, covert instructions to Toby:

"Listen quickly. This is the way things stand. You know Sean's a Pinkerton, but you don't know how I came to be here. You just came out to warn me because Sean was asking around town about me and you weren't sure whether I was in trouble."

"Right."

"I'll let Sean take it from there."

Smiling when Sean pulled up beside them, Samantha greeted him with "Hello, Unc . . . Sean. Long time no see."

Sean smiled. Samantha saw that the power of the casual smile he flashed underneath his white handlebar mustache did not match the intensity in his blue eyes when he responded, "I figured I needed to look you up, Samantha. It's been too long. I'm in need of some good company, and I figure you're the best there is."

"You're right there." As if in afterthought, she added, "You know Toby Larsen. He's a good friend. He knew you were a Pinkerton and heard you were looking for me, and he figured I should know about it in advance."

"My occupation has nothing to do with my wanting to see you again, Samantha."

Samantha almost choked at the sudden softening of Sean's voice and his half-lidded gaze. He was old, but she suddenly realized that he was still a damned sexy man! She added silently to that surprised conjecture that he must've been trouble for women in earlier days.

The thought that he still might be trouble for women lingered.

Sean said unexpectedly, "How soon do you start work, Samantha?"

"I start in a few hours. Why?"

"That'll give us some personal time together because that's what I've been wanting." He added with a wink, "Where's your room?"

Samantha hid her amazement at the side of Sean she had never seen before. She swallowed and matched his tone. "I'm staying at the Sleepy Rest Hotel if that's good enough for you."

"It's fine." Turning to Toby, he added, "I'm glad to see that Samantha has a good friend in town." Turning back again to Samantha, he said, "But I'm also glad that he isn't as good a friend as I am."

Samantha managed a smile as she rode back to town between the two men. After Sean and she said good-bye to a frowning Toby, she felt Sean's hand on her arm as he guided her toward her room in the hotel. She saw the loving glance he turned on her—until the door of her room closed behind them.

His expression changing abruptly, Sean inquired in a solemn tone she remembered too well, "All right, young lady, what's wrong and why did you ask me to come?"

They were motionless in the quiet glade in the aftermath of their lovemaking. Matt lay beside her and Jenny turned her head to look at him, wondering. Why had she never felt like this before—this magic at the sight of him and this breathlessness each time he touched her? Why was his body so newly tantalizing? Why did his gaze seem to caress her in a way it never had before? Why did those same eyes seem to see her not only as the good woman she had always been, but as the loving, tender woman she could be only with him?

Those questions silently plagued Jenny. She felt no embarrassment at their mutual nakedness. She felt no need to apologize for her slight size or her plain features because Matt had made her feel beautiful.

She had sensed his sincerity when he had loved her with tenderness and unmistakable passion. She remembered his words clearly.

"I've dreamed of this from the first moment I saw you." And *"You're the realization of a dream for me, Jenny, a dream I never thought would come true. I want to keep you with me forever."*

Nagging viciously at the back of her mind was the uncertainty she sensed in his remarks, as if he did not believe he could keep her. But she was his betrothed, wasn't she? He loved her, and she loved him in ways she had never thought herself capable of loving. That was all true, wasn't it?

Matt asked, "Is something wrong, Jenny? Do you regret—?"

"No, don't ask that question, Matt!" Sliding her hand across his lips as he turned fully toward her, Jenny whispered, "I can't bear to hear the words. But just so you'll know for sure, I have no regrets. You gave me the most memorable moments of my life—something I believed I would never have—and I love you for making me feel that way." She corrected herself a moment later. "No, that isn't right. The truth is, I just love you."

He frowned more darkly.

Aware of his sudden discomfort, Jenny asked, "Did I say something wrong? Please tell me if I did, Matt."

"Don't call me that name."

"What name?"

"Matt. My name isn't Matt. It's Tucker."

"Tucker?" Jenny attempted to smile through her confusion. Appearing conscious of their nakedness for the first time, she struggled to cover herself with her discarded dress.

"No, don't. I didn't mean to make you wary of me, Jenny." Grasping the hand that had reached for her clothing, he stuttered uncharacteristically, "I need . . . I want to tell you something, Jenny." Clutching her hand close to his lips, he continued. "Maybe this isn't the best time to tell you, except to say I didn't intend any of this to happen between us when I rode out to see you today. I intended to confess something I should have told you before—something I didn't have the courage to tell you before."

"You don't have to 'confess' anything to me, Matt. I know everything I need to know about you."

"My name is Tucker, and you *don't* know everything you need to know about me."

"I don't understand."

He said determinedly, "First of all, Matt is my twin brother."

Jenny's eyes widened and Tucker protested her reaction with a soft curse. He whispered, "Don't look at me like that, Jenny, please. I didn't mean to startle you."

Jenny attempted to rise, but Tucker held her fast. He whispered, "Listen to me before you react, please. I need that. I need to know you've heard everything I have to say before you decide what to do. Because whatever you decide, I'll cooperate with it. I promise."

136

Jenny did not speak and Tucker briefly closed his eyes. He opened them a moment later to whisper, "You do believe me, don't you, Jenny? I haven't destroyed your trust completely, have I?"

When Jenny still did not reply, Tucker continued. "If you're wondering how this all came about, Matt didn't know about me and I didn't know about him at first. I only found out recently after our mother told me the truth on her deathbed. It was too late by then, of course. The story of her love affair with Jeremy Strait and the child—*children*—that resulted from it didn't make much difference to me considering the lifestyle I had adopted. I robbed banks, Jenny. I spent the money as fast as I stole it in every manner of a dissolute life you can imagine."

He continued determinedly. "But my mother's story smarted more and more as time wore on. I finally decided that I needed to meet my father and brother. When I discovered that my father had died, that he had led everyone to believe that I never existed at all, and that he had left the entire ranch where I was born to Matt, I was furious. It didn't make any difference to me that the ranch was heavily mortgaged and that Matt had worked around the clock to keep it going. I resented him and everything he had turned out to be because he was *the chosen one*. I was determined to prove that he wasn't any better than I was. I also recognized the advantage Matt inadvertently provided by being my twin. I started robbing Texas banks and allowing my face to be seen, just to confuse people. I guess I figured I would get Matt to acknowledge me one way or the other."

Pausing for a comment that Jenny did not make, Tucker then continued. "I admit that you weren't my first thought when I learned about you. I went to town instead when I heard that the town's newest saloon woman, Samantha Rigg, was after Matt. I wanted to embarrass him and get a little for myself at the same time, but that didn't work out for me. Samantha turned me down flat every time I approached her, and Matt got me to promise that I wouldn't visit her pretending to be him anymore. I gave Matt that promise easily because in extracting that promise, he had left the door open for my visits to you. I was determined to make the best of a good thing."

Tucker saw the pain that crossed Jenny's expression, and he whispered, "I'm sorry that even occurred to me for a minute, Jenny. The trouble is, I never expected *you* to be *you*."

Swallowing, Jenny whispered with obvious resentment, "You never expected that I would be so willing . . . so needy . . . so eager for your loving."

"I never expected that you would be so honest, so trusting, so . . . good."

"Oh, thank you."

"No, don't be contemptuous of that description! I mean what I say. I had never met a woman like you, a woman who looked me in the eye, and even if she called me by a name that wasn't mine, seemed to see right down into my soul. I felt close to you, but I wanted to be closer. I needed you in ways I never needed a woman before, and my need for you seemed to grow with every meeting."

"Of course, I understand," Jenny said sarcastically. "A handsome man like you would always want a plain woman like me."

"I did! I still do!" His lips moving closer, Tucker whispered, "But you aren't plain, I told you that! The time you spent in my arms while I made love to you is burned into me. I'll never forget it. I can't."

Jenny's lips trembled. She whispered, "Let me get up, Matt—I mean, Tucker. I want to get dressed."

"No."

"Please!"

"No. I want to hold you a little longer. I want you to forgive me."

"Forgive you?" Jenny shook her head. A tear rolled toward her temple as she whispered, "I've laid myself bare to you in more ways than one. I told you I loved you and that I loved the way you made me feel. Isn't that enough?"

"It isn't . . . not now. I want you to forgive me."

Jenny locked her teeth tight, and then said, "All right, I forgive you. Now may I get dressed?"

"I want you to mean it, Jenny."

Jenny's brown eyes were moist as she whispered sincerely, "Maybe I can forgive you someday, but you're asking too much of me right now. I've been used, do you understand? I've allowed someone to make love to me who isn't my betrothed—and I admitted to enjoying every minute of it! Is there any excuse for that behavior?"

"Only that you did the same thing that your *betrothed* continued to do to you."

"Wh . . . what do you mean by that?"

"I mean . . ." Tucker's glance became more solemn. "I went to Matt's cabin just before I came here. Samantha Rigg was there, and they . . . they had been together."

"You're lying!"

"I'm not lying. I wish I were."

Jenny closed her eyes, and Tucker continued. "But once I came, things got out of hand. The feelings I had for you boiled up inside me. I wanted to make love to you, and when you seemed to feel the same, my resistance slipped away."

"Please, don't remind me how I acted."

"I can't forget it."

Refusing to meet his gaze, Jenny said with steel in her voice, "Are you finished now?"

"I don't have anything else to say."

"Then let me get up."

"Jenny—"

"Let me get up, I said!"

Tucker's restraint fell away and Jenny stood to dress. She did not realize he did the same until she turned to see him fully clothed. She said, "I'm going home now, Tucker. I'm going to tell my father that you had to go back to the ranch and couldn't stop off to see him. I'm not going to embarrass him any further than I've already embarrassed him without his knowledge today."

"Jenny—"

"In case you don't understand what I mean by that, I'll tell you more clearly. I'm not going to tell my father any of this happened—ever! I'll tell Matt, though. I could never lie to him. I'm sure he'll confess his interlude with the saloon girl, and then we'll gradually separate and go our own way without anyone being the wiser."

"Jenny, please listen to me."

"You've said enough, Tucker. Whether Matt acknowledges you or not is his business. I don't want any part in the masquerade you both perpetuated—not anymore."

Mounting, Jenny forced herself to say coldly, "Good-bye, Tucker. I hope never to see you again."

She rode off, sitting stiffly erect. She did not look back to see Tucker standing silent in the empty glade. Nor did she realize that his heart, as well as her own, was breaking.

Samantha forced a smile at the tall, white-haired man whose blue eyes scrutinized her so carefully. She knew Sean so well. The only problem was that he knew her well also. Her uncharacteristic behavior in calling him in on the case that he had worked on briefly before being called to another had surprised him. It had bothered him because he knew something had happened, especially since she had been determined to do him one better.

When she did not immediately reply to his question, Sean persisted, "I told you that you were making a mistake with your plan to prove yourself, but you didn't listen. So what went wrong, Samantha?"

Samantha hesitated again to reply. Sean was clever, astute, intuitive, and relentless. All were qualities she admired in his work, but all were qualities she now saw as a threat to Matt. Uncaring whether it was right or wrong and truly uncertain why she cared at all, Samantha knew she couldn't make the ultimate betrayal of revealing what she had learned—not yet. She had to protect Matt somehow.

She bluffed, "I'm afraid I got frustrated, Uncle Sean."

Sean's brows knit together in a frown. "I think you can forget the 'uncle' part temporarily. I don't want you to make that mistake in front of someone."

"All right, Unc—I mean, Sean."

"Now that that's taken care of, you can answer my question, young lady."

"I think you should stop calling me 'young lady,' too. That could be just as damaging."

"All right." Undeterred, he said, "I'm waiting for you to explain yourself."

Samantha responded, "Like I said, I got frustrated. I wasn't getting anywhere. I tried everything to get close enough to Matt Strait so he'd talk to me confidentially, but he resisted. It's that fiancée of his. He pretends to be so loyal to her."

"I got to admit that puzzled me, too, especially in view of the reputation of his alter ego."

Samantha barely managed to maintain her surprise at Sean's unwitting reference to Matt's *other self.*

Apparently unaware of Samantha's struggle, Sean shook his head. "The alibis that Strait provided were solid. There was no way I could shake the statements of the different people who claimed he was with them each time the robberies occurred."

"I was determined to discover something that you had overlooked in the brief time you spent on this case. When I couldn't, I figured I'd ask for your help."

Sean regarded her more closely. "That doesn't sound like you, Samantha. You don't give up."

"I didn't give up. I asked you to come."

Sean eyed her silently.

Samantha asked, "Are you angry with me, Unc . . . I mean, Sean?"

"No."

"Then what?"

"I'm wondering what you think I'll be able to do that I didn't do before."

Suddenly remembering a man who had passed through town earlier in the month, Samantha said, "A fella named Josh Harden showed up at the Trail's

End a while back. From what I heard, he comes every year, but this time he mentioned that he didn't like the new people living in a cabin north of here. He said they ran him off, contrary to the common hospitality in the area. Strange thing is that when I inquired casually about them, Josh said 'those fellas' had moved into the area within the last year, since they weren't there the last time he came through. He didn't think they had a woman with them, either, which made me suspicious. A woman would be part of the mix if they were homesteading, and since the timing was right, I figure it could be the gang Pinkerton is looking for.

"What made it all sound more plausible," she continued, "was that one of the fellas Josh talked about sounded enough like Strait to be Strait. I figure maybe that fella was mistaken for Strait somehow, and that's where the confusion came in. It seems worth investigating, but I don't have time to do it since at present I'm conducting a covert search of Matt Strait's property in the hope that I'll find some evidence that he's the one we're looking for."

Sean quizzed, "If you've found all this out by yourself, why do you need me? It would be just as easy to finish your present investigation, and then ride out to look for this cabin if you need to. That's the way your pa would do it."

Samantha's jaw tightened at Sean's reference to her father. She glanced away briefly, then faced him to say, "Truth is, I'm not sure I can hold off the regulars at the Trail's End too much longer, considering what they're thinking."

Sean's face reddened. "If any of them fellas have taken anything for granted—"

"Not yet they haven't." Samantha could not help being amused by Sean's indignation. She continued. "I'm just not sure that I can manage the masquerade necessary to investigate freely much longer. I'm not a Pinkerton yet, you know. I don't have that protection."

"Such as it is," Sean mumbled. He then inquired more directly, "Where is this cabin supposed to be?"

"I don't know."

"You don't know?"

"Josh said it's somewhere north of here."

"This is a big state, Samantha." Sean's lips twitched. " 'North' doesn't pinpoint the location too well."

"I'm sorry. That's all I've got, so you can see what I'm facing."

Again, Sean did not respond.

Samantha swallowed nervously. The story was thin. She didn't know if she'd take it seriously herself, but she hoped Sean would.

Sean asked unexpectedly, "What about this Toby?"

"He's all right. He's a friend."

Sean nodded. "I'll look into it."

"What does that mean?"

"It means I'll look into it."

With no recourse, Samantha said, "You'll let me know what you decide to do. I mean, I'll have to figure something else out if you can't follow through."

Sean did not reply. Instead, he turned toward the door. He paused only long enough to ask, "When do you have to show up at the Trail's End?"

"In about an hour."

He nodded and walked out.

The door closed behind him and Samantha released a relieved breath. So far, so good.

He didn't like Samantha's story. He had the feeling she was lying for some reason, and his gut was never wrong.

Sean walked across Winston's main street, careful to avoid the potholes. He had been in countless towns like this one before, and they were all the same—or close to it. One of their similarities was that the town saloon was the rumor mill, which Samantha had learned early on was the only place to be.

Sean stepped up onto the boardwalk outside the Trail's End. He pushed open the swinging doors. Yes, these towns were all alike and he knew exactly what to do.

"Say, ain't you that Pinkerton that came through a while back?"

Sean looked up at the mustached bartender as he stepped up to the bar. The fella had a good memory. "That's right."

"Ain't caught those bank robbers yet, huh?"

"No, we haven't."

"Too bad." The bartender put a drink in front of him when Sean motioned for a glass. "I guess Pinkertons can't always win."

"I guess not, but I figured I'd check on a rumor I heard recently about a fella named Josh Harden."

"I know him." The bartender smiled. "He comes through once or twice a year. He don't work regularly no more. That bad leg, I guess."

"Samantha said he almost got run off this time by some new people."

"Yeah, he talked to Samantha for a while, but I think I overheard him mention that."

"Samantha told you about Josh?"

Sean turned toward the small brunette who had unexpectedly joined his conversation with the bartender. He raised his gray brows and replied, "Samantha's an old friend, so I stopped off at her room for a while to catch up on old times." He sighed. "It was a real comforting experience."

Helen frowned.

"Josh didn't like it too much, being run off, I mean."

Sean frowned at the fellow who walked up beside the brunette and responded in her stead.

"Josh is used to being treated real hospitable by everybody in the area, and he didn't care who heard him complain about the newcomers."

"Is that right?"

"I guess Josh has a right to feel that way, considering all the work he did for the ranches hereabouts."

Sean nodded and tossed back his glass casually. He returned it to the bar noisily and said, "I guess that's true. Did he mention where these new folks were? Down south somewhere?"

"I think he said the cabin was somewhere up north, but he talked more to Samantha than he did to me."

"Up north, huh?"

"I didn't hear no direction," the brunette added.

"I did," the bartender chimed in. "He said up north."

Sean smiled, a friendly smile. He said offhandedly, "Where's Toby, by the way? He was real friendly to me. He seems to welcome strangers."

"I guess so, but to be truthful, he's kind of choosy," the bartender responded. "He's a real friend to Samantha, though."

Sean nodded. "So I guess I'll be heading up north if I want to find some new information. Thanks."

Slapping a coin down on the bar, Sean tipped his hat to the brunette and walked out the doorway.

He ascended the staircase of the Sleepy Rest Hotel a few minutes later and knocked on the familiar door. When Samantha answered wearing her saloon-girl clothing, he frowned. "Your pa wouldn't like that neckline."

"My pa would understand."

"Would he?" Sean shrugged. "Maybe your pa was broad-minded. I ain't." He added without giving Samantha a chance to speak, "I'm headed to scout out that cabin up north."

"Good."

"You'll be here when I come back?"

"I'll wait."

"Good." Stooping, Sean kissed Samantha's cheek and ordered stiffly, "Be good until then."

"I promise."

"I'll hold you to that."

His glance saying more, Sean started back down the hallway and disappeared from sight.

"Is he gone?"

Samantha jumped with a start and then turned toward Toby when he emerged from the corner of the hallway where he had hidden. She responded, "He's gone."

"To scout out that cabin up north?"

"Yes."

"That'll give you some time."

Time to do what? Samantha thought.

As if reading her mind, Toby responded, "You can decide what you want to do by the time he comes back." He hesitated and then continued. "I sure hope it's the right thing, too."

Samantha responded honestly, "The only trouble is that I'm not sure what the right thing is."

"I wish I could tell you, darlin', but you're going to have to figure that out for yourself. Just remember, you're going to have to live with whatever you decide for the rest of your life."

With those words of wisdom, Toby tipped his hat with a half smile and said, "I'll leave you to your thoughts."

Samantha did not move until Toby turned the corner of the hallway and also stepped out of sight.

She knew that Sean had checked up on her and that he had probably satisfied himself that she was telling him the truth about Josh Harden, and probably about Toby, too. She expected it. Checking up on details was his way of working, even though she had sensed that he was suspicious that she wasn't telling him the full truth. She was grateful that Josh had been accommodatingly vocal in his complaints and had been equally vague about the "new people." Sean should be busy trying to find them for a while . . . she hoped.

Samantha walked briskly downstairs. She emerged onto the sidewalk in time to see Sean ride off. She was alternately glad he had fallen for her ruse and sad that she had sent him on a wild-goose chase. He had rushed to town the minute he received her telegram. It hadn't mattered to him whatever else was on his itinerary. He knew her as well as her father did, and he had known something was wrong. She had come first with him from the moment of her father's death, and he took his responsibilities seriously. Though she was certain his suspicions had not all been allayed, she could not expect more of him than he gave.

But she needed to be sure what to do before she acted. She could not allow Sean's presence to push her into a hasty decision. With that thought in mind, Samantha turned and started toward the Trail's End. The bartender knew she was in town and she needed to show up for work. She needed the cover that job provided a little longer.

As much as she wanted to live up to her father's image and uphold the honor of the profession for which he gave his life, she knew she couldn't reveal Matt's secret—not for her own benefit.

Could she?

Jim pulled Helen back from the Trail's End window, where they saw Samantha watching Sean ride out of town. He drew her toward an empty table. They were seated when Samantha entered and walked toward the bar to a hail of greetings from the fellows standing there. She turned unexpectedly toward him and smiled with a nod.

Jim felt suddenly saddened. She wasn't jealous. She didn't have that kind of feeling for him—but he did, for her.

Turning toward Helen, Jim said softly, "Thanks for following my lead when that Pinkerton fella was talking to the bartender."

"Samantha is my friend, too."

"I figured whatever Samantha told him—for whatever reason—she needed someone to back her up. I figured I owed it to her to be that person."

"Me too."

"You too?"

"Samantha is kind to me. Not that the rest of the women here aren't. Not that she ever said anything, but Samantha seems to think of me in a different way. I am different from them, I guess." Helen shrugged. "I'm new to the job here. I have a lot to learn that Samantha already knows."

"Samantha's got a second sense about some things."

"She doesn't judge, and I'm glad."

Jim did not respond.

"Don't feel bad, Jim." Helen's dark-eyed gaze searched his. "Samantha is a free spirit. She isn't ready to settle down."

Jim replied candidly, "She isn't ready to settle down with me, you mean."

"No . . . no, I don't mean that!" Helen smiled encouragingly. "You're a fine man, Jim. You're more than any woman could ask for, and Samantha knows that."

"I don't know if that's really true."

"Maybe she knows she's not ready to settle down. Maybe she sees something in your eyes that she's not ready for."

"Maybe."

"Maybe she suggested that you should come to me because she knows I won't take anything for granted as far as you're concerned."

Jim saw sincerity in Helen's gaze. He smiled. "You're a nice person, too, Helen."

"Thank you, Jim. That's a compliment I don't usually get here."

Jim responded, "I don't know why."

Helen flushed. "Fellas here tell me I'm pretty. They tell me I dance real good, that I appreciate their humor, and that I'm fun to spend time with. They figure that's what I want to hear because I'm just doing my job when I'm nice to them."

"You're more than that, Helen." Jim's brown eyes warmed with sincerity. "You care about people and you're a good friend to Samantha."

"I didn't do anything that she wouldn't do for me."

"I suppose that's why I like you."

Helen flushed again. "That's another thing I don't hear often enough . . . that a fella *likes* me."

"Since we have something in common, let's drink to it."

Jim raised his glass, then emptied it with a single gulp.

"There's nobody in this saloon I'd rather spend time with, Jim. So here's to us." Helen emptied her glass also, then hiccupped. She raised a hand to her lips and laughed. Somehow breathless, she did not speak when Jim covered her other hand with his.

Matt looked out the window of Tucker's decrepit cabin as the sun began setting. He had waited for

Tucker to return, but it would soon be dark. If he waited much longer, he would have trouble seeing the trail. Besides, knowing Tucker, he couldn't be certain where his brother would spend the night.

Pulling the door of the cabin closed behind him, Matt walked toward his horse. He mounted, scrutinizing the surrounding area cautiously before nudging his horse forward. He was riding at a brisk rate when he suddenly realized where he was going.

And he knew why.

Chapter Eight

Matt rode slowly into Winston, noting that the town had an appealing quality at night with all its short-comings veiled by the shadows. The boardwalk was no longer uneven and dangerous to those unfamiliar with its terrain. The lack of paving on the main thoroughfare, and even the potholes that were to be avoided at any cost, appeared "quaint." The pretense of the French boutique with elaborate draping lit by the single, imported lamp in the window seemed interesting rather than garish. The mercantile, with its barrels and boxes lining the walkway, gave the appearance of abundance. But any serious shopper in town knew otherwise. Last but not least, the saloon's bright, flickering lights, music, and laughter spilling out onto the street were welcoming—a beacon in the dark—instead of gaudy.

The effect was totally contrary to the atmosphere that pervaded the town during daylight hours, but it was comforting in a way. Matt remembered that comfort because it had offered the only source of relief when cowboys like him were out for a night on the town.

In all, Winston was his home. Its easy familiarity was comforting.

A nagging discomfort surged to life at that thought. At least it would be comforting once he took care of something that gnawed relentlessly at his peace of mind.

Matt dismounted and tied his horse to the rail outside the Trail's End, then walked inside. His feelings anything but casual, he scanned the noisy interior, his attention coming to rest on the blonde beauty who stood at the bar surrounded by admiring cowpokes. He remembered that he had admired Samantha the first time he saw her, too. In truth, however, admiration had changed into feelings that had become stronger despite his stringent reservations.

Taking a stabilizing breath, Matt approached her. He halted behind her, knowing he had never needed to announce his arrival. He wondered if those circumstances had changed.

She had not needed to look at the doorway of the noisy saloon to know Matt had entered. She had felt him coming.

Realizing she had no choice, Samantha turned toward him. She said casually for the benefit of others, "Well, nice to see you, Matt."

"I need to talk to you, Samantha."

Matt's voice was level and deep, unlike his controlled rage when she found out the secret of his brother's dual identity.

Aware that others were listening, she maintained rigid control and replied, "I'll be happy to talk to you, Matt, but as you can see, I'm busy right now. Maybe later."

"I need to talk to you now."

"That's impossible."

"Samantha—"

"You heard her, fella." Straightening up, a thin cowpoke slurred with an edge to his voice, "She don't have time for you now. She's busy . . . with us. Ain't that right, Samantha?"

Matt's expression hardened. "Samantha can speak for herself."

"She already did. She said she'll have time for you later."

Matt was about to respond when Samantha said laughingly, "I guess if it's important for Matt to speak to me, the sooner I get it over with, the better." Matt saw the cowpoke frown before she whispered a few words to him and he suddenly grinned.

Uncertain whether he liked the idea of that whisper, whatever it was, Matt allowed Samantha to take his arm and lead him to a corner where they were afforded semiprivacy. Her back toward the bar and her expression sobering, she asked, "What do you want, Matt? I thought you said everything you wanted to say already."

Matt's anger faded the moment her gaze met his. Her eyes weren't dancing for him anymore.

He began earnestly, "I came here tonight to apologize for what I said to you, Samantha. I was angry. I didn't want to believe you came to Winston purposely looking for me. I didn't want to accept the truth that your attraction to me wasn't spontaneous, and that you weren't hit as hard when you first saw me as I was by you. When I realized the truth, I felt robbed . . . cheated somehow."

"Have you said everything you want to say now, Matt?"

Matt took a step closer. He whispered, "No, I haven't. I owe you an explanation that I was too angry to give before. I'm sorry about that. The fact is that as far as I know no one knew I had a brother for years—including me. And no one was more surprised than I was when I first found out about Tucker. I didn't know what to do about suddenly having a twin, especially since he was a wanted man—except that I couldn't betray him. You were the only thing in my life that seemed to make any sense at that point because I wanted you in a way I've never wanted another woman. And you seemed to want me. When you saw Tucker and the truth about your mission came out, it was more than I could bear."

Samantha attempted to break into Matt's ardent confession, but Matt persisted. "After you left, it occurred to me that Tucker didn't know you were connected to the Pinkerton Agency. I rode out to warn him, but that didn't work out, either. I don't know where he is right now. Only one thing is clear. I made a mistake when I sent you away. I made love to you for only one reason—because I wanted to. I need to apologize."

The saloon's noise faded from Samantha's hearing when Matt whispered more softly, "I needed to apologize because I ache inside at the things I said, and because no matter how the truth hurt, I still want to make love to you. I suppose that will never change."

Samantha swallowed past the lump in her throat that Matt's confession had raised. She couldn't tell him about contacting Sean, that he was a senior Pinkerton agent who would follow through on everything she had learned, and who, despite the wild-goose chase she'd sent him on, would be sure to figure everything out now.

She still hoped to find a way to change the situation, but sincerely doubted that she could. She couldn't tell him that, either.

She hedged. "There are things you don't know about, things that will forever be between us."

"Right now nothing stands between us, Samantha."

Samantha shook her head in silent contradiction. She explained, "I've wanted to be a Pinkerton all my life. You were my ticket into the agency. I've done things—"

"I've done things I regret, too, Samantha."

"The problem is that I'm not sure I regret those things, Matt!"

Momentarily silent, Matt responded uncertainly, "If you're not sure, I guess that could be a step in the right direction."

"I don't know if it is or not."

Silence pervaded between them until a slurring voice unexpectedly interrupted, "Are you done talking yet?"

Matt and Samantha's attention snapped toward the unsteady cowboy who had faced Matt down at the bar. Forcing a smile, Samantha replied, "I told you I'd be back, Ted, didn't I?"

"That's right. But I want you to come back now. The boys and me miss you."

Samantha heard herself reply as she turned back toward Matt, "Well, I guess we've both said everything that's to be said, anyway." She continued with forced brightness. "So good-bye, Matt. By the way, I accept your apology."

Fading into the crowd on Ted's arm, Samantha did not look back to see a stunned Matt remain temporarily motionless at her abrupt dismissal. Nor did she see him turn just as abruptly to leave the lights of the Trail's End behind him.

The hours stretched longer as the night waned. The smoke in the Trail's End thickened, and the relentless music from the piano in the corner could hardly be heard over the increasing din of slapping cards, dancing feet, and raucous laughter.

Samantha regretted not having been able to speak confidentially to Toby after her conversation with Matt. He had watched them as their conversation progressed and had waited among her admirers at the bar. She had longed for his sage advice, knowing it would give her fresh insight into a situation that was unclear at best, but the necessary privacy had been impossible.

When fatigue had eventually taken its toll and Toby left earlier, she had not forgotten the look in his eye. It had said he believed in her no matter what she decided to do. And when Toby walked un-steadily toward the doorway, the truth became sud-denly clear. She had depended on him to tell her simply that she had taken the coward's way out! She had listened to Matt's explanation and had accepted his apology without offering her own. Nor had she asked him what he intended to do about Jenny, a hard question she needed answered, even though she was unsure whether Matt's response would make a difference.

She was so confused.

Her smile jarred to artificial brightness by the slurred voice beside her, Samantha wondered how much longer her ardent fans could be put off by her manufactured excuses. She knew there was safety in numbers. She encouraged those numbers with laughing quips and timely departures to entertain in her faulty contralto. Although she truly liked most of the men surrounding her, she knew there was only one man who held any personal appeal.

The lights of the Trail's End went dark behind her as Helen, Maggie, and she made their way toward the hotel hours later. Maggie mumbled disgruntedly about going solo for the night when most of the other women had found company. Samantha had allowed Helen and Jim privacy at the saloon doorway after a brief adieu, and had suffered an assault of guilt at the thought of where Sean might be spending the night.

She tried to avoid thinking about Matt as she walked toward the hotel—whether he had taken the opportunity to apologize to Jenny, if Jenny had accepted his apology, and if they had decided to go on from there with business as usual.

That possibility cut cruelly.

"Samantha."

Samantha turned with a start toward the figure stepping unexpectedly out of the shadows. She struggled not to react when Matt continued with a half smile. "I thought I'd take another chance to talk to you."

He wasn't with Jenny.

Samantha's eyes filled with relieved tears as a hazy glow encompassed him.

She swallowed when he whispered with a question in his voice, "Samantha?"

Unable to respond, she walked wordlessly into his arms.

Toby stood in the shadows a distance away. He had been unable to sleep with thoughts of Samantha heavy on his mind. He had seen her expression when she returned from talking to Matt in the shadowed corner of the Trail's End. He had not been deceived by her smile. He had known that it wasn't over between the two of them despite things that went unspoken.

Shortly after he'd left the Trail's End, Toby realized he would not be able to sleep, not when he believed Samantha wanted to talk to him. So he had gotten up from his bed and dressed, expecting to talk with her when she was finished at the saloon for the night. But he could see now that was not meant to be.

He watched Maggie's eyes narrow when Samantha walked into Matt's arms without a word. Helen was silent as Maggie spoke sharply in a tone that brooked no argument and pulled her along beside her. He watched the two women hurry toward the hotel while Samantha and Matt remained behind in the shadows.

Toby frowned when Samantha and Matt followed the same path moments later.

Unable to decide whether Samantha was right or wrong, he was certain of only one thing. Samantha went where her heart dictated. There was honesty in that. He hoped it would be enough.

* * *

The door had barely closed behind them before Matt pulled Samantha into his arms and kissed her with familiar hunger. Sharing that hunger, Samantha returned his kiss. Feeling free and unencumbered when the impediment of her clothing fell away, she stood unashamedly naked in their intimacy. She assisted Matt's effort to shed his clothing with shaking hands. She mumbled an incoherent word when they came together at last.

Compelled by desire and as impatient as he, Samantha made no protest as they slipped to the floor and Matt covered her body with his. She gasped, unable to utter gratification when he entered her in a rush, driving hard against her. Passion soared when he plunged more deeply inside her.

Moist and ready for him, she joined his frenzy, aiding his efforts. Her eyes fluttered open as the moment approached, and she knew his tight expression reflected her own. She joined his soft cry of spontaneous joy when they reached mutual completion in a burst of light.

She did not speak when they lay breathless in the aftermath of their joining. The moment was too intimately beautiful for words—too ardently true to express.

She maintained her silence when Matt lifted her gently into his arms, carried her to the bed, and lay down beside her. She turned toward him, and their lovemaking resumed. She mumbled incoherently, enjoying each moment of Matt's painstaking care to bring her to climax again and again while delaying his own satisfaction.

She writhed at the pleasure of his touch, the sensation of his hands against her body sending her into a world of ecstasy she had never known—a rapture that was meant to be.

The loving continued.

Hours later Matt slept exhausted beside her, but Samantha's sleep was sporadic. Matt drew her closer even in his slumber, and her throat closed as his arms wrapped around her. Reality had returned, and she was stunned by what she'd felt when she saw Matt waiting for her outside the Trail's End.

Damn it all, he had misled her from the beginning! He had kept secrets from her and had betrayed his betrothal to a woman she respected more than she dared admit.

Tumultuous emotions . . . frenetic, ceaseless desire . . . the thought that time stood still when she was with him despite everything that stood between them, what did it mean?

The truth suddenly clear, Samantha swallowed the lump that had formed in her throat. She slid down to rest her head in the crook of Matt's neck. She breathed deeply of his maleness and indulged in the total masculinity and beauty of him that had enthralled and left her powerless throughout the night.

She loved him.

Yet through all his passion, Matt had never said he loved her.

Samantha closed her eyes. She determinedly ignored the tears that slid out from underneath her closed eyelids at that admission. Aware that she was helpless against her love, uncertain where it would lead, she again attempted sleep.

Sean rested in his temporary camp. He was no stranger to having twinkling stars in the night sky the only ceiling over his head, or to feeling the hard ground underneath his bedroll. Nor was he unaccustomed to the relentless searching he had halted when daylight waned.

Samantha had suggested he find the newcomers rumored to be in the area "up north" in her stead. She had said that from the information she had gained, the newcomers were possibly the bank robbers Pinkerton was seeking, but she didn't have time to search for them while she pursued current possibilities.

With such a vague location, he did not believe Samantha thought he would find them easily. That concerned him, especially since a sixth sense told him that Matt Strait held the answer to the puzzle she hoped to solve.

Yet he had followed Samantha's suggestion.

The answer to why was simple. Thomas Rigg was a friend, and the friendship between them had not been severed by death. He was devoted to Samantha with a fidelity that would not end until the day he, too, expired. He was determined to make her life complete in the meantime, whatever it took to do so.

Samantha's reaction to his appearance puzzled him. He did not believe her excuse for sending for him. She had always been independent. Perhaps she had sent for him in a weak moment and was sorry she had. Perhaps she had realized belatedly that she could solve the case by herself and didn't need him. Whatever, the die was cast. He was there. The fact that she had sent for him had galvanized him immediately into action simply because it had evinced an uncharacteristic vulnerability that had concerned him. But whatever her reason, he did not intend to leave until he was sure she was all right.

His decision reaffirmed, his mind drifted and his eyes grew heavy. He watched a cloud trail across the moon as a prelude to the sleep he well deserved.

The night darkened.

The fire in his campsite sputtered.

Nighttime fragrance rustled in the foliage around him, but Sean ignored all the familiar sounds and fell asleep.

Samantha was comfortable in the circle of Matt's arms as he lay in bed beside her. His body was warm, and a scent that was totally masculine and Matt's own filled her. She inhaled deeply in an attempt to draw it in, her tongue flicked out, wanting to taste the flesh so close to her own.

Mmmm . . . it was delicious, and she—

Suddenly uncertain if she was dreaming, Samantha snapped her eyes open and glanced at the bed beside her. In the dim light of impending dawn stealing through the blinds of her hotel room, the gaze of light eyes met her own. Matt's mouth covered hers and Samantha indulged his kiss. She took it deep inside her. After all that had happened, he had not left her. That realization gave her hope.

"I have to leave, Samantha."

Reality was hard. Unaware that she was frowning, Samantha listened as he continued. "I can't put off telling Jenny any longer. I want to be sure she doesn't hear any rumors that might be circulating before I can explain everything to her."

Reality glared more brightly.

"What's wrong, Samantha?"

"Nothing. I want you to tell her." Samantha nervously pushed back a gleaming lock that had fallen onto her forehead. "I'm just not certain what you're going to say."

When Matt did not respond, Samantha asked, "What are you going to say, Matt?"

"I'm going to tell her . . ." Matt hesitated and then shook his head. "This is hard for me, Samantha. Jenny has always been my friend. We've never kept secrets from each other."

"She's your friend and you were going to marry her?"

"I know it's difficult for you to understand, but being with a woman was previously just a matter of fulfilling a need for me. There was nothing else involved—no emotion that survived the moment. I never had an attachment to the women involved, and I thought it would never be any different. When my father died and I assumed responsibility for the ranch, I started to think differently. I couldn't let the ranch slip away. My father had worked all his life to keep it for me. It was the only home I had ever known. I had to make a serious effort to save it, and I knew I couldn't do it alone. Jenny was in the same position as I was since her father was getting old and she didn't have any brothers to take over his land."

Samantha's frown darkened at that remark and Matt explained carefully, "This is a hard country, Samantha. Without a man at her side, Jenny's life will be difficult after her father passes—almost impossible. The boundary of her ranch borders mine and her father sincerely likes me, so I figured the solution was easy. I honestly thought friendship would be enough for marriage because I had no trouble being faithful to Jenny until I met you."

Matt paused and then whispered, "Everything changed then."

Samantha's heart pounded. She waited for the words she wanted to hear, but Matt continued instead. "I have to tell Jenny that it isn't going to work out the way we planned. I owe her that much."

Samantha nodded in solemn agreement. Everything Matt had said was true. He owed Jenny the truth, yet he wasn't aware that the whole truth was that she loved him, and although she had come to Texas with another dream in mind, her hunger for him had compromised everything she had worked toward most of her life.

Samantha remained wordless when Matt stood up, naked in the dawning light. Unable to avert her gaze, she scrutinized the strong body that hard work had earned him. Always aware that he dwarfed her in height, she had somehow not realized that his shoulders were so broad. His arms and chest rippled with power as he reached for his clothes, and his legs were corded with muscle.

Samantha looked at his narrow waist. A familiar heat suffused her when her gaze followed the trail of fine, dark hair that dwindled to an area below his beltline where curls surrounded a part of him that she had briefly considered hers alone. She had worshipped his body as he had worshipped hers, so fully that he had shuddered uncontrollably at her ministrations. She remembered acutely the way he had joined his flesh to hers then, swelling inside her even more when passion assumed control. She remembered vividly the throbbing that signaled his release and the satisfaction it had dealt her the moment before she joined him.

Yet she now wondered if those moments—ingrained forever in her memory—meant the same things to him that they meant to her.

The sense of dread that she avoided in Matt's arms swelled anew. Matt hadn't asked her if she had kept any other secrets from him when she confessed her true reason for being in Winston. She hadn't volunteered to tell him about Sean, or that Toby, Matt's father's old acquaintance, knew more about his past than he realized.

Never more conflicted, never more aware that she was naked in more ways than one, Samantha drew the coverlet up to shield herself when Matt approached the bed. She remained silent when Matt kissed her. She was still silent when he closed the door behind him.

Sean didn't believe it! The abandoned cabin that had been described to him as merely being "up north" stood before him in an area that had recently been partially cleared. He had discovered its location accidentally, but sooner than anyone had believed he could.

He had awakened that morning at dawn to a day that promised to be warmer than usual. A modest breeze had rustled through the trees as he had cooked a hasty breakfast over a renewed campfire. He had then carefully extinguished the flames and resumed searching for the cabin that he had begun believing more and more was merely a figment of Josh Harden's imagination.

A brief stop at a nearby town too small to deserve a name had led him to a trail he had followed without conviction. Yet he had arrived directly at the cabin he now viewed from the protection of a wooded copse—which had to be *the* cabin.

Surprised, but too experienced to act until he was more secure in his present circumstances, Sean scrutinized the area in typical Pinkerton fashion. He noted that the few stumps in the yard had been recently cut and judged that the cabin's occupants had not been there long enough to make a true mark on the land. The partially constructed barn added to that assumption, as did the newly plowed personal garden barely visible behind the cabin. As for the ranch house itself, the windows appeared to have been recently cleaned to afford better visibility, and the doorstep freshly swept. He suspected the interior had been recently set about. The smoke rising from the chimney revealed further signs of life.

From appearances, the occupants of the land intended to stay, but he had not yet seen a living soul.

He frowned at the lack of horses or a corral to house them, of a cow for milk, of chickens that were a staple for most ranchers starting out on their own. He assumed there was a woman in the house, considering the freshly planted personal garden, but . . . something was wrong.

As if in silent response to his questions, the door of the cabin opened and a fellow about forty years of age emerged. His hair was long and he was unshaven. He motioned to someone behind him, and a young fellow in his early teens walked out into the sunshine. They started toward the barn just as a few horses from a remuda concealed in a wooded copse came into sight and neighed at them.

The young fellow laughed and started in their direction while the older man continued on toward the barn.

He noted one thing clearly. They were unarmed. It was time to make his appearance.

Riding out of concealment, Sean came to within a few feet of the men in time to see them both scramble for the shotguns lying near the doorway of the cabin.

"Don't try it!" his deep voice boomed, halting the scrambling feet as Sean continued tightly, his gun drawn. "You don't want to make that mistake."

Angry at being caught unawares, the older fellow growled, "No, you're the one who's making a mistake if you think you can take anything else from us. I'll die before I let you steal what we have left."

The younger fellow said resolutely, "You can't shoot both of us before one of us reaches a gun and brings you down."

"Let's stop this here and now." Sean's gaze

narrowed. Holding his gun steady, he said more softly, "I'm not here to rob you, if that's what you're thinking. This gun is merely to protect me from any false conclusions."

"That's what the other fellas said!"

"I'm not one of those other fellas."

"Who are you, then?"

Instinct told him not to reveal that he was a Pinkerton agent just yet. "I'm just here to ask a few questions."

"Questions? Then why the gun?"

"For protection, I said. You fellas have a reputation for chasing away strangers, and I don't want to go until I get some answers."

"So what are your questions? We're just homesteaders hoping to work the land."

Sean questioned, "Then why a race for your guns?"

The older fellow inquired in response, "What did you say your name was?"

He'd had time to better assess the pair, and now Sean felt safe in replying, "My name is Sean McGill. I'm a Pinkerton. I'm looking for bank robbers rumored to be in the area, and I was told you're likely suspects."

The older man laughed out loud, a sound lacking mirth as he responded, "We're victims, Mr. McGill, not crooks." He hesitated, then said, "My name is Harry Martin. This here's my son, Jeff. My wife, Mary, is inside."

Sean looked toward the door.

In answer to his unspoken question, Martin offered, "She ain't well, thanks to the crooks who robbed us on our way here."

Sean quizzed, "What's the matter with her?"

Ignoring him, Martin said, "I'm inviting you to get off your horse so we can talk like you said, but that's all I'm inviting you to do."

Sean dismounted and approached him. He holstered his gun. The female face at the window and the distinct glint of the rifle she held poised were the deciding factors. If she had wanted to, the woman could have shot him easily.

He didn't regret his decision as the older man started to speak.

"I'm sorry, Jenny. I don't have any excuses for the way I acted."

Matt and Jenny were alone in the ranch house. She had appeared upset when he rode up, yet his mind had wandered as he dismounted. He had traveled there straight from Samantha's bed. The taste of her was still in his mouth. Her scent seemed to follow him. Yet he was wary.

His father had loved his mother until the day he died, but he had wasted his life, and Samantha was too much as his mother had been. His father had said his mother was beautiful. So was Samantha. He had said she was charming one minute, harsh the next, and was a true asset in every saloon where she worked. It must have been true, because his mother had supported herself and Tucker, but that description fit Samantha perfectly, too. No one had to tell him that his mother had taken his father for everything he had before leaving him, either, because he did not remember a time when his father and he did not scrape by.

Although Matt knew the toll loving his mother had taken on his father, he had only recently learned the heavy toll it had taken on the twin brother he had not known existed. The truth was that he was glad his mother had never returned. He was glad he hadn't repeated his father's mistake of loving her. He was glad he hadn't had the same sad childhood as Tucker, too.

Yet Samantha seemed to mirror his mother in countless ways. Her eyes had spoken to him in a way no other woman's had before, yet that same gaze had proven devious. It had said she wanted him, although he now knew her attraction to him was all part of her plan. It had said she needed him, although he now doubted her total sincerity. Her gaze had made promises to him without speaking a word. He had given in, but now that he was away from her, he wondered if she would follow through with her silent pledge.

Yet Jenny was just the opposite. She was plain and comforting. Quiet and shy, she had never extended herself to anyone but him. To his recollection, she had never spoken an untrue word and had devoted herself to her father, and then to him.

He truly did love her in so many ways, yet he had betrayed her.

His distress evident, Matt continued softly. "I can't say what happened to me because I don't really understand why I acted the way I did. You don't deserve it."

Jenny's eyes filled with tears as Matt attempted to continue. She halted his confession with a half smile. "I understand, Matt. You were driven to do what you did because the relationship between us was somehow lacking."

"No, it wasn't! Don't blame yourself, Jenny."

"I'm not blaming myself unduly, Matt. And I truly do understand because I reacted much the same way with someone close to you."

Incredulous, Matt went still. No, not Tucker!

"I didn't know you had a twin, Matt. I didn't suspect for a moment that Tucker wasn't you."

It was true.

"He looked like you, and his voice was just like yours."

"You don't have to explain."

"I do! I was totally taken in by him, except he said things to me that you had never said. He kissed me like you had never kissed me, and then . . . then . . ."

"Tucker took advantage of you."

"No, he didn't. I gave myself to him."

Matt's anger escalated to rage. Jenny had confided in him when distraught and had been a confidante who never betrayed him. She told him things she never told anyone else. She alternately listened to his advice and advised him, and he had heard her voice over the sounds of a world that called to him in a way he only now understood. She had been a stabilizing facet of his life when it had seemed filled with unknown turmoil.

She was the loving sister he had never had.

The sister.

He implored, "Jenny, you don't have to say anything else. I understand what happened. Tucker tried the same thing with Samantha."

"But she was too smart for him. He told me about approaching her and that she ran him off, Matt—but I didn't."

"You sympathized with him. You thought he was me."

"No . . . not really."

Matt went silent.

"I didn't react the same way to him that I do to you, and I didn't understand it. He was you, but he was more than you. He wasn't like a brother to me. He looked at me in a different way. His reactions set my heart pounding. And when he confessed who he was—"

"He confessed?"

"He came to me. He wanted to tell me everything, but I wouldn't listen at first. I loved him, Matt, and I told him so. I wanted him, and he knew it. He . . . he just took what I offered."

"He took what you offered because you thought he was me."

"No . . . yes . . ." Jenny shook her head. Silky brown strands escaped her bun and Matt unconsciously tucked them back into place with brotherly affection.

"That's what I mean, Matt. He didn't touch me like you do. He touched me . . . like a lover."

"You believed you were betrothed to him."

"He said he was sorry, Matt, and I believe him. I believe him completely."

"And you forgave him."

"Yes."

"Like you forgive me."

"You didn't do anything wrong, Matt. You just followed your heart where mine didn't lead you."

"Jenny, please don't forgive me too easily."

"Do you want me to berate you, Matt? I could do that, but whatever I said wouldn't hold true. I know now that it would never have worked out between us. We like each other." She shook her head as she corrected herself. "No, we love each other, but it's a platonic love unrelated to the passion that we're capable of feeling. You'll always be a part of me, but not the part that Tucker filled so easily."

"Tucker again."

"Don't be angry at him, Matt. He's angry enough at himself."

"I doubt it."

"I believe he was sincere when he asked me to

forgive him." She added, "But I told him I never wanted to see him again."

"Why, if it was all a case of mistaken identity?"

"Because I made a fool of myself, Matt! I believed everything he said, even though I realized later that his words were prompted by the emotion of the moment, and then regretted. I invited him to make love to me, Matt, not with words, but with actions that he couldn't turn down."

"You knew I wouldn't lie to you, so you believed everything he said."

"I knew somehow that Tucker wasn't you, but I forced myself to believe he was. In my heart, I betrayed you, too."

"That's not true."

"Yes, it is."

Momentarily silent, Matt prompted, "What about your father?"

"I'm not going to tell him the truth and embarrass him unduly. When you and I drift apart and cancel our betrothal, he'll understand. As for Tucker, I told him that I hope never to see him again and that whatever you decide to do is between the two of you."

"I'll take care of Tucker."

The sound of his voice frightened her and Jenny protested, "No, Matt, please!"

"I'll do what I have to, Jenny."

"It was my fault, I said!"

"I don't agree."

Ignoring her earnest pleas, Matt tipped his hat and turned toward the door. Jenny gripped his arm in a last attempt to dissuade him, but he shook her off.

Matt knew only that she had forgiven him because *she* felt guilty—but there was only one person who deserved that guilt.

"All right, Samantha, what's going on?"

The afternoon sun was dropping into the horizon when Samantha opened the door of her room to see Uncle Sean standing there. She attempted to conceal her surprise that he had returned sooner than expected. He had apparently come directly to her room upon reaching town, judging from the trail dust on his clothing, which might have been normal considering that she was supposed to be waiting for the results of his investigation. But his expression said otherwise.

Aware that her masquerade at the Trail's End was still necessary in light of her uncertain circumstances, and that she was expected there soon, Samantha had dressed the part with a gaudy red gown and a neckline calculated to draw male glances. Sean again registered his disapproval of her apparel with a glance that she did her best to ignore.

Remorse soared as she searched his face. She hated deceiving him, especially since he had responded so promptly to her desperate wire, but Matt hadn't returned. She hadn't had a chance to talk to him, and she didn't know how to react to Sean's questions. Sean was the only authority figure she had respected since her father's death. It was still a wonder to her that she hadn't realized he was still a handsome man or that he must have been a real heartbreaker in earlier days. Despite his white hair, she knew he was still strong as an ox and that the attraction women felt toward him was probably still as strong as it had always been.

"I asked you a question, Samantha."

Samantha knew that tone. Sean had a rigid sense of right and wrong. She had borne the rigors of his disapproval in the past, and also knew that when he advised her, he was usually right.

Samantha replied evasively, "I suppose I should ask you first what you found out and why you're back so soon."

"I'm back because I found the new people you asked me to find."

"You did?" Samantha's surprise said it all before she urged, "And?"

Sean's gaze tightened. "You knew they weren't the bank robbers we were looking for, didn't you?"

"I wasn't sure, but I couldn't afford to take the chance that they were."

"Those people were victims, not thieves. They were robbed on the way here and left almost penniless. Men pretending to be weary travelers stole almost everything they had, and they were determined not to fall prey to that situation again. That's why they ran off anybody they didn't know."

"How can you be sure they told you the truth?"

"Because Martin's wife, Mary, was beaten by one of the men, and she's been afraid of strangers ever since. She hid at the window and didn't show her face, but she could've killed me with a single shot from her rifle. She didn't. I'd say that proves their story."

"Oh."

"Is that all you have to say?"

Suddenly ashamed under Sean's scrutiny, Samantha confessed, "The truth is that I never should have asked you to come, Unc—I mean, Sean. I was confused when I sent that wire. I didn't give myself enough time to straighten things out."

"That would've been all the more reason to wire me."

"I have to straighten things out by myself. That's important to me."

"I thought becoming a Pinkerton was important to you."

"It is."

"Still?" Sean asked.

"It's been a goal all my life."

"Then let me help you."

"No."

"No one needs to know I took any part in the affair."

"I'll never be sure I'm worthy of the job, then."

Sean scrutinized Samantha's pale expression with a look that she felt could see down into the darkness of her soul. He then retorted, "Well, I guess that's all that needs to be said. I'll head back where I came from."

"Thank you."

"When I'm ready."

Samantha winced. "That isn't necessary, Unc—I mean Sean."

Sean smiled knowingly. "I'll see you around, Samantha."

"But—"

Sean turned and left abruptly, without waiting for her to finish her remarks. Left alone in the silent room, Samantha realized that Sean had simply heard enough, had made a decision, and did not wait to hear what he knew would only be more excuses.

A sense of impending doom was unavoidable as the sound of Sean's footsteps gradually faded—because she knew him and she believed his every word.

"Have you seen Samantha yet?" Toby appeared anxious as he approached Helen in the Trail's End. Day was fading and he was nervous. Lack of sleep was taking its toll.

"No, I haven't. She's due here any minute, though." Helen glanced at the fellow beside her. Jim had become one of her regulars . . . one of her most welcome regulars. They had discovered they had more in common than they had ever realized. Both had had a surprisingly strict upbringing until turned out on their own at an early age by circumstances that couldn't be controlled. Both had made their way however they could, although Helen's choices had been more limited. But both had the same dreams—mutual dreams that Helen realized were becoming more and more entwined as time wore on.

However it all turned out, Helen knew she had Samantha to thank for the joy Jim brought her. She would never forget her for it, which made the small brunette only too conscious that Samantha's smiles were too forced and her reactions too sharp.

Guilt plagued her. She had seen Samantha's expression when Matt had waited for her outside the Trail's End that last time. She should have said something. Perhaps she should have reminded her that Matt was already betrothed, but uncertainty and Maggie's swift arguments had prevailed.

"I need to talk to her."

Helen ventured, "Is something wrong, Toby?"

"Nothing that can't be fixed." Toby's wrinkled face creased in a half smile—which fell the moment Samantha entered the saloon. Starting toward her, he turned back to say with a tip of his hat, "Sorry for bothering you, Helen."

Helen watched Toby's harried step, and she turned back to Jim with a frown. "Something's wrong, Jim. I'm worried about Samantha."

185

Jim's shy smile flashed. "If there's one thing I know, Samantha's got good judgment. She's the one who told me to come talk to you."

Helen's heart flip-flopped in her breast. That was the nicest thing Jim had ever said to her. She replied softly, "Thank you, Jim."

She then turned back to watch the serious conversation that commenced between Samantha and Toby. "But I'm still worried."

"You said Samantha could take care of herself, but to be honest, I'm starting to worry about her again, too."

Their conversation stilling, they watched the exchange between Toby and Samantha with mutual frowns.

"What are you going to do?"

Samantha looked at Toby's unsettled expression. She had just entered the Trail's End after speaking to Sean. Toby had drawn her immediately aside.

"I've been thinking things over, Samantha," Toby began. "I think I should tell Matt what I know about his brother."

"Why?"

"Because I think he should do what his father would want him to."

"Which is?"

"I don't know. I'm hoping Matt will."

Samantha considered Toby's concern. She had not expected this turmoil when she came to Texas.

Her life had been cut-and-dry after her father's death. Sean had arranged for her to live at school on the little her father left her. He had visited her regularly until she was eighteen years old, when she graduated with an unshakable objective in mind.

She had not anticipated when she came to Winston with her grand plan that Matt would be Matt. She had believed that her more obvious female attributes, her knack for cool logic, her inborn independence, and the skills her father had inadvertently taught her would grant her success. She had never thought that the driving desire to become a Pinkerton would be compromised so effectively when she first saw Matt, and that she would eventually be helpless against him.

Nor did she know that Matt had a twin brother whose birth had gone unreported or that Matt had never met his brother before Tucker showed up on the scene. She knew now that she had depended too heavily on the investigations of the Pinkertons who had worked the case before her and had made a mistake by dismissing misidentification of any kind.

With a familiar chill, Samantha recalled the weakness that beset her every time she saw Matt. Because of it, she had wired Sean because she had been frantic for help. Yet now faced with Sean's suspicions and Toby's sudden realization that the twin he had believed dead was alive, she was at a loss.

Aware that Toby awaited her response, Samantha

forced a smile. "I don't think you should act hastily, Toby."

Too acute to be fooled by her subterfuge, Toby asked, "Meaning?"

"Don't say anything yet."

"Why?"

"Because Matt has too many other things on his mind right now to add something else."

"Jenny, you mean."

Samantha's smile faded.

"He's going to tell her about you and him?"

She nodded again.

"Where does that leave you?"

"I don't know."

He paused, and then said with a sympathetic smile, "You don't know what to do and uncertainty ain't your thing."

"No."

"Darlin'." His expression softening further, Toby said, "I don't want to do nothing that will make you sad. I won't say nothing at all for the time being if you don't want me to. Is that all right with you?"

Samantha blinked back sudden tears. "Thank you, Toby."

"You don't need to thank me. I'm just doing my best with my second chance, is all."

Uncertain what he meant by that, Samantha blinked again. Toby did not allow her to inquire when he tipped his hat abruptly and said, "I didn't get much sleep last night. The older I get, the more sleep I need, so I'm going back to my room for a while. I'll see you later, Samantha."

Toby walked unsteadily toward the door. Samantha watched him briefly before heading for the bar where admirers were waiting.

Helen and Jim exchanged glances from their position as concerned observers. Their suspicion that something was wrong was a reality. Anxious to help, but uncertain what to do, they waited.

Matt had nudged his mount to a faster pace after talking to Jenny. His confession made, he had then been faced with Jenny's unexpected confession, and rage had overwhelmed him. Making love to Samantha had been his choice, but his brother had used Jenny's confusion at their identical appearances to deceive her. He could not allow his brother's actions to go unpunished.

Drawing his gun as a precaution when the dilapidated cabin that Tucker used came into view, he dismounted and crept up on it slowly. He peered through the window in an attempt to see inside. Aware that the effort was useless, he then burst through the doorway with gun still drawn.

The cabin was empty.

He cursed aloud, wondering where Tucker could be. He doubted that Tucker would go to town since his brother did not want to compromise his anonymity by possibly appearing in town at the same time Matt did. He knew only one thing. Tucker would have to come back sooner or later.

He waited—again.

Matt became increasingly tense as the sky darkened. It was obvious that Tucker would not return that night. Refusing to think where his brother had gone, Matt walked out the doorway and strode to the copse where he had hidden his horse earlier. He made his way slowly in the darkness, hopeful that his mount was surefooted.

Dismounting at his ranch at last, Matt settled his mount in the barn for the night, and then started toward the house. He paused, the hair on his neck rising when he saw a lamp lit in the ranch house interior. Suddenly furious, drawing his gun without thinking, Matt burst through the doorway and came to a sudden halt at the sight of Tucker sitting comfortably on his worn settee.

Tucker was the first to speak. "You don't need that gun, brother."

Matt raised a brow, replying tightly, "I'm not taking any chances."

"I wouldn't shoot you, anyway. We're brothers, after all."

Matt sneered at the statement. "You're my brother only when it suits you."

Tucker stood, suddenly frowning. "You talked to Jenny, didn't you?"

"Yes."

"She told you everything."

His finger trembling on the trigger of his gun, Matt burst out, "You're a bastard, Tucker!"

Tucker repeated, "You don't need that gun, I said. In case you're wondering why, it's because I intend to go to the sheriff to turn myself in. I just figured you deserved to know first."

"I don't believe you." Surprised by Tucker's disclosure and uncertain if he was telling the truth, Matt was also aware that Tucker wasn't armed. He finally holstered his gun and said, "You've never been anything but bitter from the day I first met you. You admitted yourself that you intended to take advantage of the fact that we're twins until I finally gave in and told the law about you. You expected me to prove that I wasn't any better than you are, and you won. Yet now that everything has turned out in your favor, you're going to the sheriff to turn yourself in? That doesn't make sense."

"You believe part of what I said or you wouldn't have holstered your gun."

Matt asked bluntly, "Why are you here?"

"I told you."

"You've lied before."

"You went to my cabin after you spoke to Jenny, didn't you? And all the time I was here. What a waste of time."

"I went to *my* cabin on an abandoned part of *my* property, you mean."

"That's right, our father made sure of that. It bothered me at first that my father hadn't thought about me since the day my mother walked out the door. But Jenny's honesty, the unabashed truth she faced so squarely, forced me to do the same for the first time in my life. When I did, I acknowledged that even if our mother did rob me of a chance for more in life, it really is not your fault. You earned the ranch by working beside our father. I didn't."

Matt's gaze narrowed. "Why the sudden change?"

"I told you. Jenny."

Matt's face flushed. "You aren't worthy to speak her name. You knew we were betrothed, and you used it against her."

"You seemed to forget you and she were betrothed when you slept with your saloon woman."

Matt drew back. "I already told you that you were right. I'm no better than you are where that's concerned."

"You're the one who really betrayed Jenny."

"And you took advantage of her in a way I never did!"

"I didn't want to, not after I met her, but when she gave herself to me that last time—"

Not allowing Tucker to finish his statement, Matt took two quick steps toward him and swung his fist with all his might. Tucker fell to the floor with blood dripping from the corner of his mouth. Matt looked down at him and urged heatedly, "Get up! Get up, damn it! You made Jenny feel cheap . . . made her hide the truth from her father for the first time in her life."

"You're a fine one to talk, considering how much time you spent in Samantha Rigg's bed." Tucker stood. "You're right. Jenny didn't deserve anything *we* did."

"I want to know one thing," Matt said as he faced his double directly. "Do you hate me so much that you'd try to compromise the only true feelings I ever had for a woman?"

"You mean Samantha Rigg, of course, because I know you don't love Jenny."

Matt flushed as he said, "I do love Jenny. I'll always love her, and Samantha isn't what you think she is. She came here to find the evidence on you . . . me . . . either one, or both of us for Pinkerton. She was willing to do anything she had to do in order to get the job done."

"So why did she run me off when she thought I was you? I gave her a second chance, but she didn't take it."

"That's why you went to Jenny, isn't it?"

Tucker raised his chin. "She didn't run me off."

Not quite believing the mirror image of himself staring back at him, Matt responded, "So you really came here to gloat."

"I came here to say that you're right, brother. I am the bastard that the good-for-nothing, bitter woman who raised me primed into action. Our mother did her best to pass those qualities on to me, while you had the advantage of a hardworking father who took the time to teach you right from wrong. I left home as soon as I was able, but I couldn't help feeling responsible for our mother. I returned often enough to help support her when time didn't treat her well."

"She was a drunk."

"She was a drunk who had every vice in the world."

Matt shook his head. "I'm sorry."

"But I'm good at excuses. Hell, I've been making excuses for myself most of my life. The truth really is that I could've traveled the straight and narrow after I left our ma behind me, but I was too smart for that."

"I'm sorry about that, too."

"Don't be sorry, Matt. Just be glad it wasn't you she decided to take with her."

Matt was startled to hear himself say, "You're still in the clear. You can get away if you want. Samantha hasn't said anything to anybody about my having a twin yet. Nobody knows . . . except Jenny, of course. She won't say anything."

Tucker frowned. "That's not what I wanted to hear you say."

"What did you expect me to say?" Matt asked flatly. "That I'm glad you're turning yourself in? I'm not."

Tucker mimicked him by repeating, "Why the sudden change?"

"I don't really know." Matt shrugged. "Maybe because you're my brother and you got a raw deal."

Tucker did not reply.

Matt surprised himself by adding, "Don't do anything yet. Let me talk to Samantha . . . to Jenny. Let me see what they have to say."

"Why?"

"Like I said, because you're my brother and you got a raw deal."

"It's too late to straighten things out for me."

"There has to be something I can do."

"It's too late."

"Give me a chance, Tucker. You never have before. I think it's time you did."

Tucker stared at Matt. Eyes so identical to his returned his stare when Matt added, "Hell, you're my brother."

Chapter Nine

Samantha awoke in her lonely bed as the sun climbed the morning sky. The night past at the Trail's End had been long and tedious despite the lively cow-pokes surrounding her. The need to maintain her masquerade until something was settled chafed sorely. Her gaze had strayed toward the door so constantly that Bart, an old standby who hadn't yet given up a fading hope, had asked her in a slurred voice who she was expecting.

She had realized then that she was being too obvious. She told herself that no man wanted a woman when she became too obvious—the way she was with Matt. No man wanted a woman who was too needy—which was the way she felt about him at present. No man wanted a woman who was willing to chuck her life's dream for him—no man, unless he loved her.

If that was what she really wanted.

Samantha had flashed Bart one of her most dazzling smiles at that point and had dipped her bosom toward him teasingly. He had been too inebriated to see that her actions were a shield for more intense emotions.

Sean had arrived unexpectedly at the saloon as the night progressed. She was amused when the fellows at the bar did not attempt to challenge his familiarity with her. Nor did they object when he drew her to a vacant table in the corner where he pretended to drink while enjoying her company. There was something about him that made everyone respect the look in his eye, and she was glad. She had needed that respite.

She knew the truth about Sean's appearance there, however. He had come to make sure she wasn't taking the case too far and extending herself too freely to the cowboys who openly hoped for more. She knew he had spent the day engaging the conversations of anyone who would talk about her and about Matt, that he had heard all the rumors circulating about them . . . and Jenny, and that he needed more insight into the case.

It occurred to Samantha that although they made a good pretense at being more than friends, there was a comfort between her and Sean that made conversation almost incidental. Yet she had been unable to avoid the feeling that there wasn't a moment when Sean wasn't actively trying to figure out from her responses what she *hadn't* told him.

He had left eventually, taking the bottle he had

paid for with him and promising to return. She had known he had taken the bottle to disguise the fact that although they had spent considerable time together, it was almost full. She had gone back to the bar sincerely grateful to be away from his subtle questions.

Toby had come by later, but only briefly. He had joined her amidst her retinue and had drunk and laughed. Yet she had the feeling that he, also, was waiting.

Well, so was she.

She hadn't been able to get out of the Trail's End soon enough.

As Lola, Maggie, Helen, and she had walked toward the hotel after the Trail's End closed for the evening, Samantha searched the shadows, hoping.

But Matt had not come, and she said a lonely good night to the girls when they reached her door.

In her present solitude as the shadows of early morning played against the worn furniture of the room, Samantha avoided recollection of the loving past. Instead, she forced herself to explore the situation facing her.

She loved Matt, but he had never claimed to feel the same way about her. She knew that he adored the excitement between them and he was enamored of the sight of her, the taste of her, the need for more that was always present between them—but she was uncertain if the emotion he felt for her constituted the same love she felt for him. She wondered if he thought of her constantly throughout the day; if he had begun fantasizing that everything about her would be his alone; if he was concerned for her future in a world of uncertainty; if he had started imagining the day when they would awaken each morning knowing that they would be lying side by side with a sense of completion they could only get together. She wondered, finally, if he had begun thinking of a future with her.

She then wondered what she would do if he did—and if he didn't.

Her continued confusion was deadening.

"One step at a time, Samantha—and remember, what's done is done."

Her father's advice returned to mind—as appropriate to her present situation as the day he first offered it. Samantha realized that no amount of berating herself would make a difference.

Tears momentarily filled her throat. Her father had always been good at clearing a path for her.

With a deep breath, Samantha threw back the coverlet and moved the few steps to the washstand, where a fresh basin awaited her. She remembered more of his sage counsel.

"If you're uncertain, go straight to the horse's mouth."

Wearing riding attire a short time later, Samantha walked into Toby's livery. He looked surprised to see her.

"Do you want me to saddle your horse up for you again, Samantha?"

"I do."

He waited for her to tell him where she was going. Finally taking pity on the old man, she offered, "I'm going for a ride."

He waited.

"I have some things to settle."

He waited longer.

"I haven't decided where I'm going yet, but I expect to come back in time to be at the Trail's End tonight."

Finally responding with a half smile, Toby said, "I don't pretend to know it all, so you don't have to tell me where you're going, Samantha. I just want you to be safe."

Samantha replied soberly, "Don't worry, Toby. I'm armed in more ways than one."

Patting the small derringer she wore on her belt, Samantha rode out remembering Toby's final words:

"Take care. This is serious business that you're involved in."

The sun had risen to the midpoint in the sky when Samantha reached the ranch house she sought. No sound came from the barn, and there were no horses in the corral. There was no activity in the yard and no signs of life other than the smoke that trailed from the chimney. The steady column rising there indicated that someone was home to feed the fire, however, and Samantha approached with uncertainty gnawing at her insides.

Samantha dismounted and tied her horse to the hitching post just as the door of the house opened. She looked up, took a determined breath, and spoke.

"We met once before, but the outcome wasn't too pleasant. I hope we can speak more dispassionately this time."

Samantha regarded the thin, plain young woman who stood framed in the doorway. Jenny responded with unexpected candor, "Things have changed since the last time we talked. There are things we need to straighten out. Come in, please."

Samantha raised her chin as she walked into the house. She heard the door click closed behind her as she observed the main room. A kitchen of sorts with open shelving and a metal stove filled one corner. A rough table and chairs that were apparently home-made filled another. A settee, two chairs, and a worn, native-design rug defined the area where occupants obviously relaxed at the end of the day in front of a soot-blackened fireplace. The bedrooms were behind closed doors, but the house was otherwise silent. No one else was home.

Samantha turned toward Jenny. "Your house is homey and warm and obviously reflects your personality."

Jenny did not reply.

Samantha heard herself explain more generously than she had originally intended, "In case you're wondering, that was a compliment."

Jenny stood still, silently confirming all that Samantha had first assessed. Her brown hair in a bun, her features unremarkable, her figure thin almost to the point of emaciation, Jenny was not the epitome of any man's desire. Samantha knew, however, that *she* was. Yet it was Jenny whom Matt had asked to be his wife.

That thought stung, causing Samantha to begin with a tinge of harshness. "Has Matt explained anything to you?"

"If you mean that you and he have been together? Yes, he has."

"Refusing to accept the ambiguity of Jenny's words, Samantha asked frankly, "Together? By that do you mean—?"

"I mean fornicating."

Samantha frowned at Jenny's choice of words. Somehow knowing the answer to her next question, she asked flatly, "And you forgave him?"

"Yes, I did."

Disappointment surged, but Samantha swallowed it with determination and asked, "How do you expect to proceed from here?"

"The way you would proceed, I imagine."

"The way I would proceed?" Emotion mounted as Samantha replied, "I would've been shocked and then infuriated if Matt told me he had betrayed me."

"I wasn't."

"You weren't shocked or you weren't infuriated?"

"Neither."

"Why? Because you had heard rumors about Matt and me?"

"I knew the reason Matt had strayed from the moment I first saw you on the street. You're beautiful and feminine even now, without the makeup and clothing of a saloon girl to gild your appearance. I know I'm plain. I knew immediately that I couldn't compare with you."

"You compare in other ways, though."

"I told myself that I did when I first approached you. I told myself that same thing afterward when Matt came to me and said all the things I wanted to hear. He said all the rumors were true, but he said he regretted straying and asked me to forgive him. I told myself that I believed him and that whatever had happened, he had come to realize how much he loved me. When I saw him again, my love for him was stronger than it had ever been. I told him so."

Barely maintaining her feet, Samantha responded, "That's why you forgave Matt for everything."

Jenny blinked.

Forcing herself to continue, Samantha raised her chin and asked, "What about your betrothal?"

"It still stands."

The defeat of those three words hit Samantha

hard. She finally responded, "That's what I came here to find out."

Jenny frowned. "Matt didn't explain any of this to you?"

"It's of no consequence." Samantha forced a smile. "I appreciate your honesty."

Turning, Samantha walked out through the doorway and mounted. She rode away before Jenny could formulate a reply.

Samantha was out of sight of Jenny's ranch house when the first tears began to fall. They fell faster as she rode, wetting her cheeks and clouding her vision until she was forced to draw off the trail and halt before continuing on.

Taking deep breaths, Samantha dried her cheeks and attempted to stem the flow of tears. What was wrong with her? Hadn't she truly expected as much? Wasn't she grateful that Matt had decided on Jenny instead of her and had freed her from indecision?

The sound of hoofbeats turned Samantha abruptly toward the path as a mounted rider broke through the foliage. Drawing his horse up beside her, he asked, "Samantha! I heard someone, but I didn't expect it to be you. I was on my way to talk to you. What are you doing here?"

It was Matt . . . or was it?

Samantha stared at him and asked bluntly, "Which one are you?"

She saw his expression harden. "I never thought I'd have to answer that question for you."

"Tell me, damn it! Are you Matt or Tucker? Although I don't really think there's any difference between you."

"You're trying to make me angry."

"I'm trying to be truthful! You're both deceitful. You both did your best to get me into your bed, yet only one of you succeeded. Which one are you?"

"Unless I'm wrong, you wanted me as much as I wanted you."

Samantha's resistance faded. She knew which brother he was. Actually, she had known the moment she saw him.

She said with surprising control, "I spoke to Jenny."

Matt's expression darkened.

"I wasn't willing to wait any longer. She gave me the answer I was seeking."

"Did she? I doubt it." Matt's full lips tightened into a straight line. "Jenny doesn't know you and she's not the type to spill her emotions out for anyone to trample."

"I didn't want to trample them. I just wanted to know where I stood."

"And you couldn't wait for me to tell you."

"No."

Surprising her, Matt offered with unexpected softness, "I'm sorry, Samantha. I would have come right back, but there was something I needed to do first. I wanted to tell you myself and not hurt Jenny any further."

His concern for Jenny struck a match to her emotions, and Samantha felt control slip away. "You didn't want to hurt *her* any further?"

Aware that her voice had become shrill, Samantha took a deep breath. She attempted more impassively, "I expected you to come back last night. I waited. Then I hoped, but even hope grew dim when you didn't show up as the night wore on. People were laughing, joking, and smiling all around me. I was, too, on the outside, but inside I grew more and more tense. I didn't expect you to tell me that your betrothal to Jenny still stands."

"Is that all she told you?"

Samantha was unable to reply.

Stepping down from his mount in a fluid movement, Matt pulled Samantha from her saddle and cradled her in his arms. She struggled against his embrace, but he held her close against him. His superior strength finally overwhelming her, Samantha stopped resisting to hear him whisper, "I'm so sorry, Samantha. There's only one thing I'm sure of at this moment." His light-eyed gaze held hers. "I love you. I guess I always will."

Samantha went still in Matt's arms.

"Jenny didn't tell you everything. She couldn't, I suppose, because she could barely tell me."

"She said she forgave you, and that your betrothal still holds true."

"Jenny forgave me because she believed she had done the same thing. Tucker—"

Aghast, Samantha whispered, "He didn't impersonate you with her, too?"

Matt's light eyes filled with pain. "Tucker confessed who he was after Jenny and he had lain together."

Samantha closed her eyes. Tears squeezed out from underneath her closed lids at the humiliation Jenny had suffered.

"I was angry when I learned the trick Tucker had played on Jenny and what had happened between them, even if he had said he was sorry."

"Too late," Samantha mumbled. "It was too late then."

"I told Jenny it wasn't her fault, but she wouldn't hear me. She said you had seen through Tucker when he tried the same thing with you, and you had run him off. She said the truth was that she allowed Tucker to deceive her because he said everything she wanted to hear."

Samantha's question was a foregone conclusion. "Then she forgave him, too."

Matt paused before continuing. "She told me she didn't want to embarrass her father by telling him any of this. She said we could allow our betrothal to stand temporarily, then just fade away. I was so angry with Tucker that I didn't argue. I just stormed out of the ranch house to find him. The funny thing is that when I finally caught up with him—"

Samantha stroked the pained lines of Matt's handsome face when his voice drained away. He said by way of explanation, "He's my brother, Samantha. I know as sure as I'm standing here that I would've been him if my mother had decided to take me with her when she left instead of Tucker."

Samantha's stomach tightened and her throat filled. She kissed his mouth and whispered to him soothingly, knowing it would be senseless to refute his statement. He mumbled incoherently as she kissed his eyelids, knowing he hated himself for having had opportunities that Tucker didn't. She felt the brush of his thick eyelashes tickle her lips, but she kissed his self-deprecation away. She didn't want to hear him berate himself. She didn't want him to say he would have been a thief if he had been in Tucker's place, because she knew instinctively that it wasn't true. Yet she couldn't tell him that. She couldn't strip him of every speck of sympathy for his brother.

Uncertain when the look in Matt's light eyes began to change, Samantha continued her comforting kisses until they gradually became more and moved down the column of his throat to cover the chest she had stripped free of his shirt. When her hands moved to his belt, Matt remained still no longer.

Unconscious of beams of afternoon sunlight warming her naked flesh in the minutes following, she felt only Matt's mouth against hers despite the hard ground of the wooded copse underneath her back. She experienced with raw delight his trailing kisses as they moved to her breasts and heard only his rapid breathing as his ministrations increased. She felt his body harden as he pressed it tight against hers, then heard his gasp when he entered her.

She held him close, hoping the time would never come when she would have to let him go. Yet she knew in her heart even as he filled her that time and circumstance might interfere, allowing the beauty of that moment never again to be recaptured.

Labored breathing filled with endless glory . . . sweet satiation that came in a wild burst . . . Matt throbbing to stillness inside her . . .

Trembling in the aftermath of their intimacy, Samantha turned toward Matt still holding him tight. His lips found hers and she accepted his kiss— until it became more again, and she stopped thinking anything at all.

"What's wrong, dear?"

Aware that she had been unusually quiet when her father and his men returned from working the herd, Jenny regarded her father silently. Both Lefty and Mark had gone to the bunkhouse earlier than usual after supper with the excuse that they had chores to perform. She had been grateful for that because she had the feeling she would be unable to bear another moment of their questioning glances despite their obvious concern.

Jenny realized belatedly that she could not avoid

her father's questions any longer when he said, "You were quiet yesterday, and you're even quieter today. That's not like you."

"Everybody knows I'm not a talkative person, Pa."

"Maybe you're not talkative with most people, but you usually tell me whatever is on your mind. You're not doing that now, and I feel uneasy."

Jenny tried to smile. "I don't know what you mean."

"That's what I mean, Jenny. You always know what I'm trying to say, even when I don't say it right. We've always had that connection between us." He took two steps closer, stroked an errant brown strand back from her face, and whispered, "Don't change that now."

That gesture, so similar to Matt's, ripped at Jenny's composure.

"Maybe I don't want to talk. Maybe I don't want to tell you that your daughter isn't the person you thought she is."

"My daughter is everything I ever wanted her to be." Frowning, Randolph Morgan added, "But she's also a woman with a woman's feelings and with limitations that are totally different from mine. I might not fully understand those limitations, but I love her enough to try."

"Don't say any of that if you don't mean it, Pa."

"I mean every word, darlin'."

"Oh, Pa." Her facade cracking, Jenny walked

into her aging father's waiting arms and sobbed, "I let you down."

"Tell me how you let me down, Jenny."

"Matt and I . . . we . . ."

Randolph took a breath and then asked, "Are you trying to say you two lay together?"

"No. It was someone else."

Jenny felt her father stiffen. She heard his harsher tone when he asked, "What do you mean it was someone else?"

"It's a secret, Pa."

Jenny felt her father's restraint before he said more quietly, "Have you ever known me to betray a secret?"

"No, but—"

"Well?"

"Did you know all along . . . were you aware . . ." Jenny halted and then said in a rush, "Did you know that Matt has a twin brother?"

Her father's obvious shock was his only response.

"You didn't know, then."

"Are you sure?" Randolph asked incredulously.

"I'm sure now. The two of them look exactly alike. As a matter of fact, I couldn't tell them apart."

"Oh, Jenny."

"But I didn't know until Tucker confessed who he was. To be honest, I didn't want to believe it was true."

"Jenny."

"I'm sorry, Pa. I let everybody down."

Confused, aware of her agitation but unwilling to remain silent, Randolph probed softly, "Tell me what happened, Jenny—but slowly, please. You know an old man doesn't get things as quickly as most."

Her brown eyes tearful and her expression sober, Jenny started to speak.

She was still standing opposite her father when she was finished at last. With an attempt to conceal his angry astonishment, her father said, "I . . . I can't believe this." And then, "Matt knows what happened?"

"I told him and he stormed out of here yesterday. I haven't heard from him since."

"What did he say?"

"He said . . ." Jenny took a breath. "He said he'd take care of Tucker."

Randolph nodded, satisfied at that.

"I begged him not to do anything he'd be sorry for, and everything is far from settled. Our betrothal still stands for the time being, but that's all I know—except that although Matt and I love each other, it's not the kind of love we need in order to marry."

"The love between you two would grow into more."

"No, it wouldn't because there's somebody else—for both of us."

"For you both?"

"For me it's Tucker, Pa. Even though I know now

212

he lied to me, he melted me with everything he said. I knew then what had always been missing from Matt's and my relationship. Afterward . . . after he confessed who he was, he begged me to forgive him. I said I did, but I didn't mean it and he knew it."

"And Matt?"

"Every rumor you've been hearing about him, the same rumors you tried to shield me from, are all true."

"You mean about the saloon woman."

"It wasn't his fault, Pa. Neither of us recognized what was missing between us until now."

"But for you it wasn't missing with Tucker?"

Jenny's gaze silently pleaded his understanding as she explained, "I don't know what to say except that Tucker was Matt on the outside—handsome, protective, sincere. He was everything that made me proud to be chosen by him, but he was different in a way that set my heart pounding—in a way that set me afire like Matt never did."

Randolph did not reply, and Jenny added simply, "I'm sorry, Pa."

"Don't be sorry, Jenny." His lips tight, Randolph forced himself to say, "You only told me the truth. I don't know what to say in answer to all this except that you're a woman, and you have to suit yourself. I can only ask you to be honest with everyone concerned."

When Jenny appeared confused, Randolph said

flatly, "You said Tucker didn't believe you, but if you really meant what you said about forgiving him—and I'm not saying you should or that I would—don't let pride assume control. Pride passes, darlin', but regret doesn't."

Jenny still seemed uncertain and Randolph clarified, "Matt will settle things with his brother, but I have faith in your judgment. You said Tucker is Matt's twin. If he's anything at all like Matt, he's the kind who won't think less of you for your truthfulness."

Jenny looked at him.

"I didn't say what you expected to hear, did I?"

"No."

"I just want you to be sure that there's not more to this story than even you realize now that everything appears to be out in the open."

"But it isn't yet, Pa. Nobody knows that Matt has a twin. Even Matt didn't know about Tucker until he showed up."

"Now I know what you mean about it being a secret." Frowning, Randolph continued. "But it's still up to you, Jenny. I won't say anything for the time being. Just think over what I said. Whatever else happens, being truthful is never wrong."

His daughter nodded and went to her room, closing the door behind her. Randolph's expression slowly fell. He brushed away the few tears that he could not restrain and attempted to restore his control. He hadn't said much to Jenny because she had taken his breath away—but he knew one thing for sure.

If Jenny, Matt, and his brother, Tucker, didn't straighten things out among them—he would.

Aware that they had lain together until the afternoon sun was well past the high point, Samantha and Matt spoke very little while dressing. Their passions momentarily sated, Matt said thoughtfully, "Give me time to work things out with Tucker before you do anything, Samantha. He's my brother. I can't abandon him."

Samantha nodded.

"I'll get back to you as soon as everything is straightened out."

Samantha nodded again, then added, "I'm sorry, Matt . . . about everything."

Lifting her into his arms, Matt kissed her thoroughly and then slipped her onto the saddle and promised, "I'll settle things as quickly as I can."

Samantha gripped her reins more tightly when Matt slapped her horse's rump and set her off at a canter. Winston came into sight on the horizon at last, and Samantha could avoid the thought that tormented her no longer.

She had made a mistake calling in Uncle Sean because he was a man of principle who was dedicated to the law. She could no more ask Uncle Sean to betray his principles than she could ask the same of her father—yet Uncle Sean might inadvertently be the downfall of them all.

She still hadn't told Matt that she had sent for Uncle Sean; she'd been unable to find the words. She also hadn't told him that Toby knew he had a twin. She didn't know what he meant by working things out with Tucker, either. She was certain of one thing only. Uncle Sean wouldn't wait if he found out the truth.

Chapter Ten

Jenny rode with a sense of purpose she did not truly feel as the sun set. She had remained in her room to think things over as her father suggested and had emerged less than an hour later. She had then mounted and had ridden off before either her father or the ranch hands might say anything to change her mind. She had known what she needed to do.

Jenny breathed a relieved sigh when the Double S ranch house came into view. The light in the windows meant Matt was home. She was grateful that his hired men were away and she wouldn't have to face them. She had never become adept at the excuses that would have been necessary. She just wanted to explain to Matt that she had told her father. She owed him that.

Jenny drew up outside the ranch house and dismounted. Her step came to a halt when Matt appeared unexpectedly at the door. She walked inside without a word and turned toward him when the door closed behind them.

"What are you doing here, Jenny?"

Jenny's throat closed with sudden awareness. "You aren't Matt, are you?"

"No."

The appearances of the two men were almost identical, except that Tucker did not wear the belt buckle Matt had worn every day since his father's death. Jenny saw the simple irony there. Jeremy Strait had found a way to make his sons distinguishable from each other even though he was dead.

But Jenny knew she would have known Tucker anyway.

"You didn't answer me, Jenny."

Jenny could not immediately reply. Why was Tucker all that she had ever wanted Matt to be? Was everything she saw in his gaze that she had never seen in Matt's—like desire and a soul-shaking need for her—merely a figment of her own yearning?

"Jenny?"

"I wanted to talk to Matt."

Tucker took a step back. "He's not here. He said he had something to do. I don't know where he went."

"I wanted to tell him first that I had spoken to my father."

"So you told your father what happened. Somehow I knew you would."

"Then I was going to find you."

"Why did you want to see me?"

Jenny began uncertainly, "I wanted to say I'm sorry because I left you without clearing things up between us."

"I think things were clear. Matt told me before he rode off that your betrothal stands."

"For appearances only."

Appearing truly stricken, Tucker whispered, "I'm sorry about that."

"I'm not." Aware that she had startled him, Jenny took a forward step. "You misrepresented yourself, Tucker. I'm not glad you did that. Nor am I proud that I gave myself to you, but you actually did both Matt and me a favor. You made us aware that it could never have worked out between us as we planned."

"Don't say that, Jenny."

"It's true. I know that now, and so does Matt."

"Jenny . . ." Regret shone brightly in Tucker's gaze. "I didn't come here to complicate your life— truly I didn't."

"Why did you come, Tucker?"

"I came—" Tucker sighed. "I guess I came because I was jealous of Matt. He had every opportunity that I wished I had had—a childhood he could look back on without bitterness and a future given to him by a father who cared. I was determined to make him suffer for it. But it didn't work out the way I thought it would."

"What do you mean?"

"Everything went crazy from the first minute I

met Matt. I knew he was my twin, but to see someone with my face stunned me. Then I started feeling different than I expected. I didn't get the enjoyment that I had hoped for in making Matt miserable, so I went a step further. Rumors about the new saloon woman and him were rife, so I decided to find out for myself. I figured she would be easy pickings."

"She wasn't, but I was."

"It wasn't that way, Jenny."

"You didn't expect everything to be so easy with me," she repeated.

Tucker's voice dropped a notch lower when he explained earnestly, "Everything stopped for me from the day I first met you."

"You didn't expect me to be so plain, or so needy," she insisted.

"I told you, I didn't expect *you* to be *you*—so honest, so straightforward, never the coquette. The possibility of being other than truthful and understanding never entered your mind. Nor did I expect you to look at me with such trust. No one ever did before and it infuriated me that it wasn't really me you trusted. I became more and more jealous of Matt, but I maintained the masquerade because you had touched me in a way no other woman ever did. I tried to resist you. I even tried to tell you the truth, but in the end, I just wasn't strong enough until it was too late."

Jenny remained silent and Tucker continued. "I

betrayed your confidence, Jenny. I can't forgive myself for doing that."

"Even if I do?"

"Your forgiveness—if that's what you're offering—isn't enough for me."

"What is?"

"I did something even I can't tolerate. For that reason, I need to forgive myself."

"What do you need to do in order to accomplish that forgiveness, Tucker?"

"I suppose I need to wipe my past clean to begin with—to change what I am into what I wish I was. I'm a thief, Jenny. I'm a wanted man."

"I'm offering you the forgiveness you won't give yourself, no matter how you feel. I said I forgave you before. I didn't mean it then, but I do now."

"You're not talking to Matt."

"I know that."

"I'm not like him."

"I know that, too."

Beginning to shake, Tucker whispered, "You'd better get out of here, Jenny. With all the good intentions in the world, I don't think I'm strong enough."

"Tucker—"

"Get out, Jenny, please."

"Tucker—"

"Leave!"

Jenny managed a shaky smile. "Thank you for being honest with me."

Again, Tucker did not reply.

Unable to say a word in farewell, Jenny turned and within minutes was mounted and had turned her horse back on the trail. She did not look back to see Tucker come to the doorway to watch her ride off. She did not see his obvious longing, or hear him mutter, "That's right, get out of here fast, Jenny. I know I'm not good for you, but nothing can stop me from wishing I were."

Jenny rode back home, certain of only one thing.

Tucker didn't want her.

Samantha paused outside Sean's hotel room. She was due back at the Trail's End. She knew she could not afford to end her masquerade there yet, but she needed to talk to Sean.

Affixing a smile on her elaborately made-up face, Samantha knocked hard on his door. Sean's automatic frown at her saloon-woman veneer changed into an uncertain smile when he said, "Well, this is a surprise."

Samantha walked inside and turned to face him when he closed the door behind her. She said, "I came here to ask you again to leave, Sean. As much as I appreciate your prompt response to my wire, I admit to making a mistake when I sent for you. I'm asking you again to let me handle this case on my own."

Samantha felt Sean's blue eyes scrutinize her carefully. She fought to maintain a confident facade when he said, "I told you I'd leave when I was ready."

"I need you to leave now. I need to know that I don't have you as a backup in case things don't go as I plan."

"No."

"No?"

"Are you surprised that I said no to you outright, Samantha?"

"Yes . . . no . . . I mean—"

"You're not telling me everything."

"I am!"

"No, you're not, and I'm not leaving until you do."

Samantha stared at Sean, incredulous at his intuitiveness. How could she explain that birth records gave no indication that Matt had an identical twin who had committed the bank robberies? Sean was a Pinkerton. He would not believe Matt had not known that Tucker existed. He would refuse to accept the tangled circumstances that had evolved, too. Nor would he give her the time she needed to figure out what she should do with that knowledge.

"Uncle Sean . . ." Not bothering to correct herself, Samantha blinked back frustrated tears and whispered, "I'm asking you to leave . . . not because I don't appreciate everything you've done for me but because—"

"I won't leave."

"Uncle Sean!"

"Don't call me uncle, either, unless you're going to reveal your masquerade."

"I can't yet."

"And I can't leave yet, either."

Samantha was suddenly angry. "I'm sorry I sent for you! I'm sorry you came! I want you to leave. Can I make that any clearer?"

"If you tell me the truth."

All trace of anger leaving her as quickly as it had come, Samantha whispered, "Nothing I can say will make a difference, will it?"

"No."

Suddenly sobbing, Samantha threw herself into Sean's waiting embrace and hugged him. She struggled to regain control and said, "I'm sorry, Uncle Sean. I didn't mean half of what I said."

"I know." His arms tightened consolingly.

"I didn't mean to hurt your feelings."

"I know that, too."

Samantha noted that Sean's eyes were unnaturally bright, and regret surged even deeper. "Just forget I came here tonight, all right? Forget everything I said. This whole thing . . . it just has me confused, that's all."

"I know, but I can help you if you'll let me."

"I—"

"But you want to figure things out yourself." Sean's expression softened. "That's all right with me. I'll just hang around until you do."

Disengaging herself from his embrace, Samantha

wiped her face dry and said with a half smile, "The truth is, although I tried hard, I didn't expect you to agree. You're such a dogged Pinkerton."

"Yes, I am."

Sean's halfhearted smiled faded when the door closed behind Samantha and he said to the empty room, "And I'm so much more."

Twilight darkened the afternoon sky when Matt rode up to the Double S ranch house at last. He frowned at the sight of a familiar horse tied up in front. He was prepared when he opened the door.

"I thought you'd be gone, Tucker." Matt closed the door behind him.

"I gave you the time you asked for in order to think things out. Now I figure it's time to turn myself in as I intended."

"I thought we agreed to wait before making irreversible decisions."

"The truth is that I'm looking at things from another perspective now. The law will discover you have a twin brother sooner or later. No matter what I thought at first, it won't do me any good to involve you in my affairs, and I don't want to be dodging the law forever."

"Why the change of heart?"

"Is that what happened to me—a change of *heart*?" When Matt did not reply, Tucker shrugged and laughed. "I suppose you can blame Jenny for that."

"Don't even speak her name." Matt's expression stiffened. "I haven't forgotten what you did. Just because I haven't done anything about it doesn't mean I excuse you in any way."

"That makes two of us, so I guess we are more alike than we think." Tucker added after a moment, "Jenny came here to see you while you were gone."

"You didn't—"

"No, I didn't pretend to be you, if that's what you're thinking. Besides, I don't think Jenny would be deceived again."

"She's not stupid, even if you did treat her as if she were."

Tucker frowned at that thought. "I suppose I might react the same way about what I did if I were in your position—but I'm not, and I resent what you said. I didn't treat Jenny as if she were stupid. I never thought that was true for a minute, especially since she accomplished what others failed to do."

"Which was?"

"She made me face myself honestly. Whether I want to admit it or not, that last day when we were together had a lot to do with it."

Matt took an angry step toward him and Tucker said, "Hold your horses, Matt. I'm just trying to say that Jenny trusted me. I was ashamed of what I did afterward—no matter how weakly I reacted at the time—which is something I thought I'd never hear myself say. I can't forget the look in her eyes when I confessed who I was. That look haunts me."

Obviously fighting his own reaction, Matt said through clenched teeth, "You're such a bastard, Tucker."

"You're right, but I didn't intend to be a bastard with Jenny. It just happened."

"I know, it just happened because Jenny and I have a lifelong history together and she thought I was you."

Their positions suddenly reversed, Tucker said, "You have a lifelong history with Jenny, huh? That's why a saloon woman managed to capture your fancy?"

"I told you, Samantha isn't a saloon woman."

"No, she wants to be a Pinkerton. That's the excuse she gave you for deceiving you as much as I deceived Jenny. But if that's true, she's going to tell the agency you have a twin and take credit for solving the case. If that's true, it's just a matter of time for me."

"She won't do that before telling me first."

"Is that why you slept with her, so she would feel obligated to tell you what she intended to do before she did it?"

"I slept with her for the same reason you slept with Jenny—because I wanted to. You said yourself that we're more alike than either of us thought we were."

Suddenly irate, Tucker said, "Yes, but you didn't steal from hardworking people so you could carouse like a drunken fool. You didn't search out fellas who thought the same way you did so that with a gang, you could make more easy money than you did alone. And you weren't arrogant enough at the time to think that you were smarter than everybody else because of it all."

"Maybe not, but if I was raised the way you were—"

"Don't say that, either. That's just an excuse. I need to believe in you, not only because Jenny believes in you, but because I need something to hold on to."

"I think Jenny believes in you, too, Tucker," Matt said sincerely. "She obviously sees something in you or nothing could have convinced her to act the way she did."

"You already gave the reason for that. She thought I was you at the time."

Matt shook his head. "I know what I said, but I also said Jenny isn't stupid."

"Maybe she became confused because I was honest with her for the first time in my life."

"Honest?"

"About the way I feel about her."

"What's that supposed to mean?"

Tucker shook his head. "Funny you should ask me that now." Avoiding a response, he said simply, "The answer is simple—maybe too simple."

Matt considered the voids in Tucker's reply and finally responded, "I think you should tell her you intend to turn yourself in."

"Why?"

"Because she would do the same for you."

"No, she wouldn't. Not now."

Matt was suddenly angry. "Why? Did you say something else that hurt her when she came to see me, Tucker? If you did—"

"I told her to leave. I didn't trust myself if she stayed any longer."

"You didn't trust yourself?"

Tucker asked belligerently, "Can you say you honestly trust yourself with your Pinkerton woman?"

Matt's expression tightened before he replied, "That's my problem, but I do know Jenny's going to suffer if you don't explain what you're going to do. She needs that confidence. That's the only way she can come to terms with what happened."

"Better she should suffer now than—"

"Jenny doesn't deserve to suffer at all!"

Unable to dispute that comment, Tucker shook his head as Matt added, "You spent your life running away from things. Are you going to add this to the list?"

"This is different."

"No, it isn't."

Tucker opened his mouth to respond, but nothing emerged. Momentarily immobile, he studied his brother's sober expression—the face so similar to his own reflecting a truth he struggled to deny. Taking the time only to snatch up his hat, he ended their conversation abruptly by saying, "It's getting dark. I'm going back to my—or rather, to your—cabin to sleep."

"We haven't settled anything."

Tucker left without replying.

The sun rose in a clear morning sky as Tucker waited concealed in a wooded copse outside the Circle O. He had slept poorly the previous night after his volatile conversation with his brother. He had awakened knowing Matt was right. He needed to speak to Jenny.

The Circle O wranglers had eaten the breakfast Jenny had cooked and had finally mounted and turned their horses to ride out for the day's work. He waited until the sound of retreating hoofbeats faded. He wasn't sure what he was going to say, but he knew how being unable to forgive himself felt. It was an ache deep inside that he could not dismiss, and a sense of failing not only himself, but also the one person who could share his future. He could not bear the thought that Jenny would live with that feeling, too.

Tucker nudged his mount into the cleared yard as soon as it was silent again. Jenny was standing soberly at the door when he dismounted. He said as he approached, "I have to talk to you, Jenny."

Jenny did not budge from the spot. "Am I mistaken, or did you insist that I leave the Double S yesterday?"

230

"I did—for your sake as well as for mine—but I thought things over when my mind was clearer and there are things I need to say."

"All right." Jenny stepped back. She closed the door behind them, but didn't invite Tucker to sit down. "Say what you want to say."

Tucker turned to face her. "I'm sorry, Jenny."

"You said that."

"But I didn't explain why."

"I think you did. You couldn't help yourself. I expect that would be true of most men if a woman offered herself as openly as I did."

"You didn't offer yourself to me, Jenny. You offered yourself to Matt."

"I didn't offer myself to Matt," she corrected with hard-edged honesty. "I offered myself to you."

Tucker's semismile was sad. "It's the same difference."

"No, it isn't. The full truth is that I knew something was different about you from the beginning. I had never felt about Matt the way I felt about you. You looked the same on the outside, but I could sense something different on the inside." She laughed self-derisively. "I was correct there, but I tried to tell myself that you and I both had discovered a part of ourselves that we hadn't realized existed before. I deceived myself purposely, but you didn't deceive yourself. You only deceived me."

"I did deceive you, Jenny." The admission was

difficult. "But I want you to realize that it wasn't your fault, so you can forgive yourself."

"Self-forgiveness is overrated."

"No, it isn't. I know that now. I might have believed that was true if I was still the person I once was, but I know now how important it is. The real truth is that the satisfaction I received when I thought I was being smarter than most honest people faded quickly. I was already dissatisfied with my life when I learned Matt existed. That's probably why I got so angry."

Jenny was about to interrupt, but Tucker continued purposefully. "I want you to forgive yourself because everything that happened is my fault. I came to Texas expecting revenge on my brother to restore that satisfaction, but it didn't work out that way. Then I met you."

Tucker paused, his face reddening before he added with considerable difficulty, "I love you, Jenny—and this is me, Tucker, saying those words. I asked you to leave me yesterday. I chased you away because I could feel control slipping away. I wanted everything to be right between us even though I knew it couldn't be. I wanted you to forgive me even though I knew you shouldn't. I wanted to believe we could go on and make a future together—even though I knew that could never be."

Aware that Jenny's face was whitening, Tucker took a step toward her and then said softly, "The truth is that I'm not good enough for you now, and I know it."

"Tucker . . ."

Tucker started to shake as the cold in Jenny's gaze slowly changed. He continued. "I can't forget the hardship I caused—especially now that I can truly appreciate all the hard work that went into the meager savings that I stole. And I can't offer you a future while the law is on my trail."

"Tucker, are you telling me the truth?"

"I am now when it's too late."

"But it isn't too late! Don't you see? You're a different person than you were before."

"Maybe, but that doesn't change what I did."

Jenny whispered, "What could prison hope to accomplish that you haven't accomplished already?"

"Punishment."

"Punishment doesn't really change anything, either."

"I can't make retribution for what I did at this point except through punishment for my crimes."

"Tucker, what do you want me to tell you?" Jenny's eyes filled as she took a conciliatory step toward him. "Do you want me to tell you that you're bad and you can never truly change? I know that isn't true. However you feel about me, your actions in coming here prove you're sincere and you're concerned about how someone else feels for the first time in your life."

"That's only because I love you."

"Don't say that again. You don't love me."

"Don't tell me how I feel, Jenny. You've made me care about the hardship I caused, and you've made me wish I could wipe it all away."

"Your past made you the person you are."

"My past made me a person who isn't good enough for you."

"That's foolishness."

"No, it isn't."

"You're Matt's brother."

"Matt, again."

Jenny could not restrain a smile. "That's what Matt said about you."

"Did he?"

Jenny paused. She finally responded, "He said that when I told him I love you."

Tucker went still. His full lips twitched and he swallowed tightly. He took a breath and then said softly, "You felt that way when you thought I was Matt."

"I never really thought you were Matt."

"Jenny, please. I only came here so you could realize that I did what I did because I wasn't strong enough to turn you away."

"I wasn't strong enough, either."

"Don't say what you don't mean, Jenny."

"Unfortunately—fortunately—I'm uncertain which, I mean those words sincerely."

"You're sure?" Tucker took a tenuous step.

"That's one thing I've never been surer of."

"Jenny—"

Closing the final distance between them, Tucker pulled Jenny tightly into his arms. His mouth covered hers and her lips separated under his kiss. He was still holding her close when he raised his mouth from hers to see light shining in Jenny's eyes again— and he realized that it did shine only for him.

He kissed Jenny's eyes closed then and felt her eyelids flutter under his lips. His kiss warmed as it covered the planes of her face with true hunger, as he tasted the shell of her ears, and claimed her mouth again at last.

A sudden fear dawning, Tucker raised his head. Had he understood only what he wanted to hear? Did Jenny truly want him—Tucker, the man he had always been, as well as the man he was now?

Tucker stared down at Jenny, but saw only the light of love shining brightly in her brown eyes.

Tucker clutched her closer. His Jenny—she was his alone.

Mason Light turned toward the smaller man who had entered the abandoned cabin where they had stopped. They were exhausted and in unknown country. It was the middle of nowhere as far as he was concerned, and he didn't like it. Of medium height, with small, tightly set features and several days' growth of beard on his pointed chin, he was wearing clothing that was liberally spotted from past days' indulgences. He said gruffly to his companion in a voice that reflected his frustration, "What did you learn?"

"Tucker rode this way, all right. He's been robbing small banks in this area pretending to be his twin brother and confounding the law, but he didn't do nothing as big as we did together. He probably wasn't getting much." The smaller man removed his hat and wiped the sweat from his prematurely balding head with a dirty hand before saying, "I don't understand it. We was doing fine. We didn't have no problems with the law, and all of a sudden he disappeared."

Mason sneered. "I figure he's up to something big now that he knows he has a twin to cover for him, and I want to be part of it. I figure I deserve it, being's I was with him before he found out he had a twin in the first place."

"You mean *we* deserve it."

"Yeah, that's what I mean." Mason looked at his cohort unappreciatively. He didn't like being corrected by a man of inferior intelligence, especially when he was uncertain why he had gotten mixed up with the fellow in the first place.

Mason continued. "Tucker's not the kind to share, though."

"Yeah, but—"

"I'll just have to make sure he tells us—or else."

Reggie Larks's round face glowed. "That's what I like to hear, that Tucker ain't going to mess with us."

Mason looked at the smaller man scornfully. "Maybe he'd mess with you, but he won't mess with me."

"We're partners, ain't we?"

Mason smiled abruptly. Reggie made him feel smart. Reggie wasn't like Tucker, who always made him feel stupid. But Tucker had needed them in order to rob the bigger banks where there were bigger paydays. That had made up for it all—until now, when he couldn't understand what Tucker really had in mind when he disappeared.

Mason sneered at that thought. Reggie and he were the only ones who knew Tucker had learned belatedly that he had a twin brother, and Tucker had been livid when he found out. Tucker had absentmindedly mentioned using his twin to confuse the law, which he apparently had done. That was a good idea that could have been great if he had made them a part of the action. But he hadn't, and he wasn't going to get away with it.

"Tucker is in the area. That's for sure, even if he didn't tell us the name of his pa's ranch so we could catch up with him."

"It don't matter anyway," Reggie added. "It ain't hard to follow Tucker's trail with him robbing banks all the way here and putting the blame on his brother."

"Yeah, and blaming it on his brother," Mason repeated with a laugh. "And that's how I'll find him."

"You mean *we'll* find him."

Mason darted Reggie a dirty look at his insistent correction. "That's what I said."

Mason added silently, *But when I do find him . . .*

The trail to the Double S Ranch was now familiar to Samantha, but she rode it without confidence as morning dawned. Matt and she had made love the previous day. The encounter had been spontaneous. In the afterglow, she had been reassured all was well between them, yet her euphoria had subsided when she had ridden back to town and realized that nothing had been settled. She still hadn't told Matt about Sean or Toby—secrets that weighed heavily on her mind. Matt was in danger. Sean was a diligent Pinkerton bound to figure out the truth, and Toby was always looking out for her safety. He could decide at any moment that the secret of Matt's twin was too dangerous to keep.

She needed to warn Matt. Matt's hired men would return in a few days and privacy would be difficult from then on. It was now or never.

That thought in mind, Samantha rode out into the ranch yard just as the house door opened and Matt emerged. His broad shoulders were erect and his muscular frame tight. His Stetson was pulled down low on his forehead. He looked at her strangely, with an unexpectedly sober attitude. She supposed her heart would always jump a beat at the sight of him, but the question if he would always feel the same about her was never clearer.

That question was prominent in her mind when Samantha said cautiously, "I need to talk to you, Matt. We didn't do too much talking the last time we were together, and there are some things I need to clear up."

His expression inscrutable, Matt made no comment other than to say, "I wasn't expecting you this morning. I need to work in the north pasture, but we can talk first."

She dismounted to see his light-colored eyes burning into hers as he asked, "What did you want to say?"

Samantha had not intended their conversation to take place on the porch of his ranch house in the light of early morning, and with Matt eager to get moving. She said hesitantly, "You obviously have something else on your mind. We can talk later."

"Now is as good a time as any."

No, it wasn't, but Samantha proceeded. "I have some things to tell you that I didn't mention before."

She paused, waiting for Matt's reaction. When there was none, she continued. "There's a new fella in town—Sean McGill. I suppose you've heard about him."

Matt went still. "The nosy fella who has been asking a lot of questions?"

Samantha stiffened. "I sent for him. He was my father's friend."

"Your father . . . the Pinkerton."

"Sean is a Pinkerton, too."

Matt did not respond, but his gaze tightened.

"Sean pretended to be an old friend when he saw I was masquerading as a saloon woman, but it's not wholly true. I've always called him Uncle Sean and I sent for him when I was frustrated and didn't seem to be getting anywhere on the case—before you and I were together. Sean was slightly involved in the investigation until Pinkerton assigned him elsewhere. I knew he would come when I asked, but I regretted sending for him as soon as I sent the wire."

"Why are you telling me now?"

"I didn't tell Sean anything. I just asked him to leave because I wanted to finish what I started, but he refused. He knows I'm hiding something. I never could fool him, and he's relentless. He'll find out about your brother. He's a real danger."

"Is that all?"

"No."

"What else?"

"Toby Larsen knows you have a twin."

"You told him?"

"He was your father's friend when he was younger," Samantha responded quickly. "He knew about your mother and father and about her pregnancy, but he seems to be the only person who knew she had twin boys."

"Why did it take him so long to figure out the whole mess?"

Samantha asked incredulously, "Do I hear a note of doubt in your voice, Matt?"

Matt repeated his question: "What took him so long to make the connection?"

"Toby figured your twin was dead, just like your father did. When your father got involved with raising you and trying to save the ranch, years passed and Toby and he went their separate ways. Toby forgot all about it for a while."

"Why didn't he say something when he remembered?"

"Because I asked him not to."

"You asked him?"

"Matt—"

"But now that we're . . . close, you're telling me."

She didn't like his tone. It was almost as if he were trying to get her angry as he continued. "You're telling me about your two 'friends' who pose a danger to the secret my brother and I wanted to keep."

"That's right."

"How can I be sure you're telling me the whole truth now?"

Samantha took a step back. "How can you say that after . . . after yesterday?"

"You're a good actress."

Samantha was astounded at his sudden change of attitude. If she didn't know better—

"It's me, all right, Samantha—Matt—just in case you're wondering."

And he could read her mind, too.

"You said you loved me yesterday, but you're a different person today," she said.

"That was yesterday."

Momentarily silent, Samantha asked, "What happened to change things between us?"

Matt did not reply.

"What happened?"

Matt maintained his silence.

"Matt—"

When he still did not reply, Samantha said solemnly, "I came out here to tell you about Uncle Sean and Toby. I did what I had to do. I'm going back to town now."

Samantha remounted and looked down at Matt briefly before nudging her horse forward. She paused after a few minutes on the trail to look behind her. Matt had not followed her. And she wondered—where had it all gone so suddenly wrong?

He had handled it poorly, and Matt knew it, but the previous day had gone badly for him after leaving Samantha. He had spoken to Tucker and realized that he would most probably get involved in his brother's troubles with the law. It was then that he acknowledged to himself that he needed to put distance between Samantha and himself in order to keep her out of the debacle.

He had not arrived at that decision lightly. Samantha was not a Pinkerton yet. She did not have a Pinkerton shield to protect her. Tucker regretted involving him in his robberies, but the result was the same. The situation was already complex, but with Sean McGill and Toby Larsen suddenly part of the mix, it was too dangerous to take a chance.

Matt stared at the empty trail that Samantha had followed back toward town. He had accomplished what he wanted. He had forced her to take a step away from him. Somehow he had not realized that the accomplishment would leave him destitute.

He wished there had been another way, but Samantha was stubborn. He had thought the situation through, and simply asking her to maintain a distance until he figured things out would not work.

He was still in the yard when the sound of hoofbeats caused Matt to glance in their direction. Startled, he saw Jenny and Tucker riding his way. He did not speak when their horses came to a halt beside the porch, or when Tucker lifted Jenny down from the saddle. He saw Tucker's deference when Jenny whispered to him. He noted the look that passed between them when Jenny slipped her hand into his.

The first to speak, Jenny said simply, "I want to tell you that Tucker told me he intended to turn himself in to the law. To be honest, I'm uncertain how everything came about afterward, but—" Jenny's face flushed and she turned briefly to Tucker for support. "But we're together now and we realize how we feel about each other."

Jenny continued in a rush when she saw Matt's dark expression. "I know it isn't what you wanted to hear me say for many reasons, Matt. I'm also sorry if it sounds rash to you, but it really isn't. I feel like I've known a part of Tucker all my life—the part that is so similar to you. I've always loved that part. The difference is that in meeting Tucker, I finally made the connection to the man within. All the expectations that I ever had for true love were met and surpassed then. Tucker says he feels the same way. I believe him, Matt, because—well, it's as if we were just waiting for each other."

Pausing for a response from Matt that did not come, Jenny continued. "I was willing to go away with Tucker to escape the law for selfish reasons—that I loved him, that I didn't want us to be separated for whatever time the law commands—but Tucker wouldn't have it. He said I would become a part of his past that way, and he didn't want that. He said he wants to get his debt to the law paid once and for all so we don't have to hide anything anymore."

When Matt still did not reply, Jenny said hopefully, "I hope you understand all this, Matt. Tucker wants to put the past behind him before he goes on, so we can face the future together."

Matt's response was to look at his brother and ask, "Do you think that's fair—asking Jenny to wait however long the law figures in your future?"

"No, but—"

Cutting Tucker short, Jenny whispered, "It's fair for me, Matt. I love Tucker. I'm willing to wait however long it'll take because I know I can look to the future only with him. But I love you, too, and I want you to wish us well."

"Jenny—"

"Please, Matt."

Matt took a deep breath. He saw Tucker's hand tighten around Jenny's. It was a subtle gesture with great significance—proprietary, supportive, and loving.

Matt said abruptly, "If you're asking for my blessing, you have it. You know I want your happiness—but my blessing comes with a condition."

Tucker asked hoarsely, "What condition?"

"I want you to wait before you turn yourself in." Glancing toward the trail where Samantha had disappeared a short time earlier, Matt hesitated and then said, "I need to handle a few things first."

"You mean with your Pinkerton?"

"Pinkerton?" Alarm flashed in Jenny's gaze. "What Pinkerton are you talking about, Tucker?"

"You know I'd never do anything to hurt you or my brother, Jenny," Matt answered in his stead. He held Jenny's gaze reassuringly and said, "Tucker can explain everything he knows to you when I leave."

"Everything I know—which isn't much."

Matt did not respond to Tucker's comment.

Tucker said, "All right, Matt. I'll wait." Then turning to Jenny, he continued. "In the meantime, we have a lot of explaining to do to your father."

Matt watched as Jenny and Tucker rode back in the direction of the Circle O without another word.

Chapter Eleven

"Who are they?"

Helen glanced at Jim, waiting for his response, and then back at the two riders who had arrived at the Trail's End earlier. She didn't like their looks. Both men were dirty, as if they hadn't washed off the residue of the long trail behind them. Their hair hung in oily strands from underneath wide-brimmed hats that were stained with sweat. Vicious spurs were attached to boots covered with dried mud and other, more offensive substances. Their pants were baggy and discolored, and the guns on belts slung low across their hips appeared to be the only accessories that were paid the attention due them.

Maggie and Denise had approached them dutifully, but both men had turned the women down, apparently as disinterested in them as they were in the casual conversation at the bar. The only thing that seemed to hold any appeal was drinking and obtaining information—about Matt.

Helen looked at Jim where he sat beside her. His only reply to her question was a negative shake of his head when he said, "I don't know who they are, but I don't like the looks of them one bit."

Jim was sitting closer to her at the table than was necessary and he had gripped her hand reassuringly. That gesture heartened Helen, but it did not eliminate her concern.

She had noticed a change in Samantha. Samantha's frivolity—always seeming to be a natural part of her personality—had become too intense and her quips too strained, as if she was having difficulty maintaining a veneer due to crack at any moment. Helen couldn't bear the thought of that. Samantha was still special to her—the person who had sent her the man of her dreams.

Helen felt Jim's grip tighten, and she flushed. She didn't mind being second choice with Jim, especially since he had said he liked her—and especially since she believed him.

"You're worried about Samantha, aren't you, Helen?"

"Yes, I am."

"Me too. I figure those two are asking too many questions about the only fella that Samantha's really interested in."

"Then you don't care that Samantha—?"

Helen halted abruptly and Jim smiled. "No, I don't care about Samantha in that way anymore. But that don't mean that I don't care about her at all."

"I care about her, too."

"I know."

Suddenly aware that their mutual caring was another bond they shared, Helen smiled. But that smile fell when the two men sauntered arrogantly toward the Trail's End's swinging doors with satisfied sneers and an obvious destination in mind.

"Where do you think they're going?"

Jim shook his head.

"I don't know what to do."

Jim's response came slowly. It was accompanied by a deep frown as he said, "Right now I don't think we have any choice but to wait and see what happens."

Samantha walked across the lobby of the Sleepy Rest Hotel in full saloon-woman regalia. She had donned her gold satin dress and the heavy makeup of the trade. She had reviewed her confession to Matt about Sean and Toby in her mind again, but could not truly account for the reaction she received.

Despite her initial anger, she had hoped Matt would regret sending her away. She wanted to start over without influences of the past if that was possible, but she was only too aware that she could not afford to make any drastic changes in the masquerade she had established. Uncle Sean could not be found at the moment, and Toby would probably show up at the Trail's End to see her sooner or later. Only at the Trail's End bar—where nothing in town passed unnoticed or unreported—could she be kept current on whatever was happening without becoming obvious.

Samantha continued toward the Trail's End with a smile and a confident walk that she did not feel. Yet she sensed something was wrong.

Samantha entered the Trail's End to the gratified calls of the fellows at the bar. Her responsive smile was immediate, but it was Helen and Jim's advance toward her—the two friends she had firmly established—that caught her eye. Their expressions stopped her cold.

Halting at the doorway when they reached her, Samantha listened as Helen spoke and Jim supported her comments. Refusing to react outwardly to their obvious concern, she dismissed their anxiety, but sauntered to the bar to speak a necessary word to the bartender and fend off the protests of the men there before leaving.

Rushing directly from there to the livery stable, Samantha was annoyed when the hired man that Toby had left on duty didn't seem to know where Toby had gone. Still wearing her saloon costume, she mounted with difficulty, knowing she could not take time to change.

Matt paced with indecision. The sound of his booted footsteps echoed in his silent ranch house as confused thoughts continued to deluge his mind. Tucker and Jenny had left together. Their appear-

250

ance as a couple had stunned him almost as much as Jenny's decision to wait however long it would take for Tucker to pay his debt to society. Yet they now faced the even more difficult problem of explaining that situation to Jenny's father.

Matt shook his head in silent distress. The old man would find it as hard to comprehend as he did. Adding to that problem would be his automatic anger. It would all take a heavy toll on the aging man who had become almost a father to Matt since his own father's death.

Yet his reaction to Samantha's confession about Sean McGill and Toby haunted him. He had known the situation was dangerous for her and had made the decision to remove her from its complexities in the only way he could. He had done what was necessary in light of the obstinacy so typical of Samantha's personality—but that didn't mean he liked it.

In truth, Samantha's confession that Sean McGill was also a Pinkerton and that she had sent for him had taken him by surprise. He could not allow McGill to take Tucker in before his brother could do it himself.

With that reality darkening his brow, Matt realized that everything depended on whether Samantha had been completely honest with him about Sean McGill—whether she was working with McGill. Despite everything between them, he was still unsure.

He also needed to warn Tucker that although he believed their birth had been a secret to everyone, Toby was aware of the truth.

He was certain of only one thing. However it turned out, he would keep Samantha safe.

With that thought in mind, Matt checked the gun in his holster, grabbed his hat, and slammed the ranch house door closed behind him as he moved toward his mount and the Circle O.

Samantha's casually upswept hair fell into moist ringlets that bobbed against her neck as she urged her mount forward at a gallop. Her satin gown was ringed with sweat, and the high-heeled shoes she had worn to the Trail's End fit poorly in the stirrups as she drew up in front of the Double S ranch house at last.

Ignoring the ripping sound that accompanied her descent from the saddle, Samantha felt only distress when she saw no movement inside the house. Still hopeful, she rushed in and called Matt's name. When there was no response, she ran to the barn, stumbling on the uneven ground and ignoring the mud that stained her dress when she did. She went still when she saw Matt's mount was gone.

Panic surged higher. From the descriptions Helen had provided, the two suspicious strangers had obviously traveled hard, had too many notches on their guns to ignore, and were too interested in Matt for safety. Without her knowledge, Helen had also perfectly described the two men reported to have aided Tucker in his bank-robbing spree prior to coming to Texas.

The strangers had left the saloon obviously satisfied with the information they had obtained. That caused her the most concern. If they were indeed Tucker's former cohorts, if they had come to find Tucker about some unfinished business, and if they were as threatening as they appeared to be, she needed to warn Matt that they were looking for him or his brother.

It occurred to Samantha that in warning Matt, she ran the risk of helping Tucker escape, the same felon she had come to Winston to apprehend. Yet she knew she needed to warn Matt as quickly as possible.

Matt was not at his own ranch now, and she somehow doubted that he was working in the north pasture. In order to find out where he was, she needed to ask to the only woman Matt had ever asked to be his wife.

Jenny.

A torturous ride later, Samantha reached the Circle O Ranch, her appearance disheveled and her mount heavily lathered. She saw horses tied up in front of the house when she drew closer, immediately recognized Matt's mount among them, and was suddenly unwilling to wait a moment longer.

Samantha jumped down from her horse, pushed open the door, and burst into the house—only to stop short at what she saw:

Two Matts, dressed almost identically, with Jenny standing pale and silent in the corner of the room near a thin old man.

Uncertain, Samantha stared. Which one of them was Matt? Which was Tucker?

They were both silent.

In a sudden flash, Samantha realized silence on their parts was a deliberate ploy in light of their uncertainty about her reason for being there.

Suddenly angry, Samantha snapped, "I don't have time for games! One of you already knows that a Pinkerton is on Tucker's trail at my request. Whatever the reason for your silence, I'm telling you now that Tucker is facing more danger than anyone realizes."

The two Matts still did not reply.

Matt maintained his silence with pure strength of will. If he were to judge from her trail-worn appearance, Samantha had ridden hard to get there, yet he dared not speak. He knew she would recognize him the moment he did and he would lose any advantage her confusion temporarily granted him.

In the few moments that passed, inevitable questions harangued his mind: Could he take the chance that Samantha was telling the whole truth? He had already endangered his brother by allowing desire to overwhelm common sense. He owed his brother a second chance, yet Samantha's plight called to him in a way that was difficult to ignore.

"Which one of you is Matt?" she demanded again.

Matt's heart pounded when Samantha drew closer. Scrutinizing them both more carefully, she then walked up to him and whispered, "Tell me now, was it all a lie, Matt?"

Matt looked down at her, revealing the hunger in his light eyes. Everyone in the ranch house was so intent on Matt's response that they failed to hear a scraping sound before the door broke open to reveal two armed men.

The taller man warned, "Stay where you are, but drop your guns—now!"

Sidearms thudded to the floor and Samantha cursed under her breath. She immediately recognized the men from Helen's description. She had arrived too late to warn Matt after all.

Mason addressed the brothers with a touch of incredulity. "You two fellas really do look alike!" He then added more threateningly, "Which one of you is Tucker?"

Tucker responded coldly, "What are you doing here, Mason?"

"I'm here, too, Tucker. I ain't invisible, you know."

Tucker ignored Reggie's comment and addressed Mason. "I thought I left you behind in Oklahoma."

"You did, but Reggie and me figured you was up to something too good to miss out on, considering what you left behind, so we followed you."

Jenny whispered, "Tell them to go away, Tucker."

"I didn't ask for your comments, lady!"

Tucker responded stiffly, "She wasn't talking to you."

"Well, ain't that something?" Mason appeared amused. "Tucker is all protective of the lady. Damned if that don't beat all!" His expression suddenly sobering, Mason sneered. "Whoever she is, she ain't got nothing to do with us and I don't want her to say nothing. If she don't shut up, I'll shut her up."

Tucker took an aggressive step. "You'll have to shut me up first!"

"I'm holding a gun, too, Tucker," Reggie added.

Mason turned with a snarl. "Shut up, Reggie. Tucker ain't talking to you. Besides, it's your fault that we got lost coming here. I ain't forgetting that."

"Don't tell me to shut up." Reggie flushed with obvious embarrassment. "And you only asked me where the ranch was after you was already lost. Besides, if it wasn't for me, we never would have heard about Matt's betrothed and wouldn't have come here."

"Yeah, yeah . . ."

"It's true, ain't it?"

"No, it ain't true, but this ain't no time to argue the point, neither!"

Reggie replied hotly, "I'm getting sick and tired of you always acting like you're smarter than me."

"Well, I am, ain't I?"

Reggie's finger tightened on the trigger of his gun as Tucker broke in opportunely. "Shut up, both of you. Let's get something straight. You wasted your time coming here. The only reason I came was—" He hesitated, shot Jenny a glance, and continued. "I didn't come to Winston to make money. I'm going to give myself up."

"What?"

The single word erupted in unison from his two former cohorts as they stared at Tucker incredulously.

"You heard me," he replied.

Mason shook his head. "Wait a minute. You ain't Tucker. You can't be."

Tucker smiled. "You're not so sure anymore, are you?"

Mason replied, "No, I ain't, but there's one way to find out. Turning his gun, he pointed it at Jenny.

Both men jumped forward.

Mason warned them back and said, "I can see that ain't going to work. I guess I chose the wrong woman." He turned his gun toward Samantha.

"Wait a minute!" both men shouted simultaneously, but the panic in Matt's gaze turned Mason toward him to say, "So all the rumors about Tucker's brother and his saloon woman are true."

"But you still aren't sure," Matt replied.

"Yes, I am—now."

The conversation progressed heatedly, too heatedly for Mason to notice at first that Matt was maneuvering Samantha behind him protectively until he warned, "I told you not to move."

"What are you going to do, shoot me?" Matt responded arrogantly. "If you do and my body is discovered, everyone will know that Tucker and I are twins."

Mason laughed. "Smart, ain't you? Except who says anybody will find your body?"

"Wait a minute!" Tucker interjected.

"Shut up! No, I take that back," he corrected. "I want to know why nobody knows about you two being twins."

Matt silenced Samantha with a glance before he said, "It's a long story."

"Yeah, I guess it is a long story because I was there when Tucker first found out he had a brother. He didn't know about you before his mother told him when she was dying, that was sure, and he didn't like it when he found out."

"I wasn't too crazy about the idea, either," Matt commented.

Mason laughed. "I guess you two were more alike than you both realized."

Matt and Tucker exchanged glances.

"Things have changed, though. It's too bad that one of you has to die."

"What do you expect to accomplish with that?" Tucker questioned tightly.

"Yeah . . ." Obviously confused, Reggie repeated, "What's that supposed to do?"

"Shut up, Reggie!"

"I told you, I'm tired of hearing you tell me to shut up!"

"You may be tired of hearing it, but you'll do what I say."

"No, I won't." Reggie seemed to swell. "Not anymore."

"You'll do what *I* say, though."

Gasps sounded in the room at the unexpected, deep-voiced interjection of the white-haired fellow who appeared in the doorway with gun drawn.

"Uncle Sean!"

Mason and Reggie turned to find a gun pointed them.

Reacting as if he hadn't heard Samantha, Sean ordered again, "Drop those guns in the name of the Pinkerton Agency!"

In a sudden flash of movement, guns barked and gunsmoke filled the room. A body thudded to the floor as others within scrambled for safety. Figures moving too quickly to identify in the grainy, gun smoke mist slipped out the doorway as the men within struggled to regain their weapons.

Matt recovered his gun first and stood up tentatively in an attempt to assess the situation. He had protected Samantha from injury by covering her with his body. He knew she was safe. He looked fearfully at the male figure on the floor just as Tucker moved out from behind the settee with his arm around Jenny. Randolph stood up breathlessly as

Matt took a few steps toward the motionless figure lying a few feet away to check his condition. He reported solemnly, "Reggie's dead."

"But where's Uncle Sean?"

Samantha's question turned everyone toward the doorway. Blood spatter and a gory trail led from the doorway where he had been standing to the place where the horses had been tied up. The other mounts had been scattered and McGill and Mason were gone.

"It looks like McGill was shot and Mason took him hostage on the way out." Matt hesitated. "I guess he figures that being a Pinkerton, McGill will be familiar with the territory and traveling with him will give him the edge he needs. I only hope he's right."

"But Uncle Sean is wounded!" Paling, Samantha continued. "Uncle Sean only came here because I sent for him. He's been like a father to me since my pa died. We have to help him."

Matt felt Samantha's genuine distress. All doubt had dissipated in that split second of time when he threw his body protectively across hers. He had known then that whatever she was, whatever she hoped to be, he loved her.

Folding her consolingly into his arms, he whispered, "Don't worry, Samantha. We'll find him."

"He's wounded because of me, Matt."

Tucker responded, "I worked with Mason. I know how he thinks. Mason was smarter than Reggie, but he isn't too bright, either. The difference is that he knows his limitations. He's going to travel as fast as he can back to Oklahoma where everything is familiar to him. That's probably another reason why he took McGill, so we'd be cautious and think twice before shooting if we catch up with him. All Mason wants now that Reggie's dead is to get away."

"But we don't know what he'll do with Uncle Sean once he gets to Oklahoma, or even how badly Uncle Sean is injured! What if Uncle Sean can't travel fast enough to suit Mason?"

"It'll be to McGill's advantage to make the effort," Matt replied soberly.

Samantha whitened further and Tucker said, "Don't worry, we'll find him, Samantha."

Tucker's reassurance fell flat until Jenny added, "I know this area, Samantha. I'll track with Tucker. I've had some experience with injuries, too, so that'll help until we can get McGill to a doctor."

Samantha looked at Jenny and then at Matt's twin. She said, "I'm so sorry about everything."

"No, I'm the one who's sorry." Tucker tightened his arm around Jenny as he said softly, "Things have changed for me, but like I said, I know how Mason thinks. The best thing we can do is to catch up with him because he won't be too patient if McGill holds him back."

"I'm familiar with the main trail to Oklahoma," Jenny offered.

Tucker shook his head. "Mason will be too exposed there. He'll want another route."

Samantha interjected, "Uncle Sean worked this territory before. He knows it quite well, even if I don't. Is there a secondary route to Oklahoma?"

"I know an alternate route, but what makes you so sure McGill will use it?" Matt questioned.

"He won't have any choice."

The silence that followed was broken by Randolph's voice when he added shakily, "You'd better get going, then. I won't go with you because I'll just hold you back. I'll take care of this fella instead." Indicating the still body on the floor, he said, "There's nothing anybody can do for him but bury him, anyway."

Matt started toward the door and Samantha declared, "I'm going with you. Uncle Sean will need to see me, and I need to explain the situation to him if he's in any condition to listen."

"You stay here. You can explain when we get back," Matt said.

"I'm going with you," Samantha repeated adamantly.

About to argue, Matt realized he was wasting time.

Waiting impatiently until the horses were recovered, Samantha was about to mount, when she turned abruptly toward Matt and urged, "Tell me everything is going to be all right, Matt . . . please."

"I'll do my best."

Matt and Tucker exchanged glances as they mounted. Unspoken was their promise to work together.

Matt traveled slowly through the forested glade with Samantha riding behind him. The plan was simple. Tucker and Jenny on one side of the secondary trail to Oklahoma, and Samantha and him on the other, would converge from different directions, hoping to confuse Mason. But with two pairs traveling together, and with only one person in each who truly knew where he was going, Matt was dubious of their success. He also knew their plain would work only if McGill could think clearly enough to steer Mason onto the secondary trail; and if Samantha were correct in believing that when she explained it all to McGill, he would believe her.

Too many ifs.

Matt looked back at Samantha. Halting his mount abruptly, aware that Tucker and Jenny were traveling unseen in the woods on the opposite side of the heavily foliated trail, he waited until she drew up alongside him.

"Is something wrong, Matt?"

"No, nothing's wrong." Reaching out unexpectedly, Matt lifted Samantha from the saddle and into his arms. He kissed her thoroughly, indulging the taste of her for long moments and knowing a longing deep inside before he drew back to whisper, "I figure I need to say it again, just in case." He paused, holding her gaze. "I love you, Samantha. Everything I said to you earlier was in the hope of sparing you danger—which obviously wasn't meant to be."

Samantha was about to reply when he hushed her. "You don't have to say anything. I just want you to know that whatever happens, my love will never change."

"Matt—"

"Shhh . . ."

Matt slid Samantha back into her saddle, his expression sober as he said, "We have work to do now."

More shaken than she revealed, Samantha sat her mount silently as they moved again through the foliage. She knew if Uncle Sean was capable of clear thought, he would take Mason to the trail they were shadowing. She also knew Mason and he would be traveling at a disadvantage because of Uncle Sean's injury, and that Matt and she would catch up with them at any time.

If they had taken that route.

Samantha swallowed convulsively. She then raised her chin as her natural self-confidence snapped into play. She knew he had taken that route and Uncle Sean would die before he let her down.

Die.

Samantha briefly closed her eyes. She snapped them open a moment later at a sound on the trail ahead. She looked at Matt. He had heard it, too, and held a finger to his lips, silencing her. She listened intently, moving forward cautiously until a harsh conversation became audible.

"Move faster!"

"I'm moving as fast as I can." Uncle Sean's voice was weak.

"I'd better reach something familiar soon, or you're going to be in more trouble than you know." His voice threatening, Mason continued. "And if I find out you lied to me and this ain't the best way for me to get back to Oklahoma without being seen, I'll make sure you regret it."

"Don't worry, I'm not lying."

"Then move faster. I want to know where I'm going before it gets dark."

Samantha looked at Matt to see him shake his head. Uncle Sean hadn't commented, but she knew from Matt's expression that Mason's request was impossible to meet.

She started to shake.

Matt frowned at her reaction, and then whistled. The sound, so similar to the warble of a bird, was returned from a portion of the trail nearby and Matt smiled. He was uncertain how he had known Tucker would return that call if he was close enough to hear it. But he knew his brother would find a way to respond.

Matt withdrew his gun from his holster and burst out onto the trail. "Put up your hands, Mason!"

Stunned by his appearance, Mason turned his gun on McGill and said, "I don't know if you're

Tucker or his brother, but I'm telling you this. Take one more step, and I'll shoot this fella just for the fun of it."

"No, you won't!" Converging onto the trail from the opposite direction, Tucker said tightly, "You may not know who's who here, but you do know that neither one of us would let that happen."

"How are you going to stop me?" Mason laughed wildly. "If you shoot me, I'll take this fella with me."

"No, you won't."

"Try stopping me."

Sean swayed weakly in the saddle.

Shots rang out on the shadowed trail at the sudden distraction.

Gun smoke caused momentary confusion as two bodies hit the ground.

Unsteady in the saddle, Samantha rode forward. Her derringer was still smoking when she dismounted and dropped it before staggering to where Sean lay on the ground. She looked up when Matt appeared beside her and heard him say, "His wound is bleeding badly. He's unconscious now, but I think he'll be all right."

Samantha glanced toward Mason's motionless figure a few yards away and saw Tucker and Jenny crouched beside him on the ground. Tucker shook his head. She then looked back at Matt to say simply, "I had to shoot Mason before he shot you."

The world began whirling strangely around her as

Samantha followed the direction of Matt's shocked gaze and saw a bloodstain rapidly widening on her bodice. She almost laughed. It was funny . . . she hadn't realized she was shot.

She felt Matt grasp her shoulders as she slumped toward the ground. She wanted to say the words she had spoken only in her mind—the words he had stopped her from returning when he said he loved her—but darkness closed in.

Samantha's fading thought was that she had waited too long.

Chapter Twelve

Samantha awakened slowly to a room filled with sunlight. She was alone. An ache in her chest still throbbed, but she knew the wound was healing well. She recalled awakening a month earlier only to hear, "Don't try to move. You were shot. You lost a lot of blood, but you're going to be all right if you don't start bleeding again."

She had been disoriented when an old man moved into her line of vision and said, "That's right. Relax."

Samantha had looked at the gray-haired fellow with the small glasses. He was pudgy, balding, and obviously middle-aged. She hadn't known who he was, but he had reassured her with eyes that smiled when he said, "My name is Dr. Jackson. There isn't a doctor in Winston anymore, so Matt brought you to my home in Foulard."

"Matt?"

"He's fine. He's outside."

"Uncle Sean?"

"He's weak from loss of blood, but he's fine, too. He insisted on waiting outside with Matt because you've been in and out of consciousness." He paused. "They'll both be happy to hear that you're lucid, but I guess I'll send Matt in first."

Samantha remembered that her eyes had drifted closed, and when she had opened them again, a familiar light-eyed gaze had held hers. Yet her smile had faded when she muttered uncertainly, "It is you, Matt, isn't it?"

"Yes, it's me." At the sound of his voice, all uncertainty had disappeared and Matt continued. "I'm sorry, Samantha. I didn't realize you'd been hit at first. I was afraid I'd lose you then, and I panicked."

"The doctor says I'm going to be all right."

Matt had grasped the hand she raised toward him and pressed it to his lips, and Samantha went still. She remembered. He had said he loved her.

Her throat suddenly filled, and she had asked, "Did I say it, Matt? Did you hear me?"

"Did you say what?"

"That I love you?"

"You said it, but you were hallucinating."

"I'm not hallucinating now."

Samantha's memory of that day was interrupted suddenly when the bed sagged with Matt's weight as he lay down beside her. She hadn't realized he had entered the room, and she smiled into his singularly handsome face—singularly, because she knew no amount of frightened confusion could ever again make her unable to distinguish one brother from the other.

She touched Matt's cheek. She traced loving lips that had whispered devotion during her recovery—words pledged from the heart.

She touched his hands—strong hands that had supported her gently as she recuperated from her wound.

Matt held her close and she remembered that he had been her first concern after the confusion on the shadowed trail. She had pushed her mount into a lunge forward without regard for her own safety when she had seen Mason point his gun at Matt. She had fired her derringer directly at Mason. She didn't clearly remember too much after that, except that a pain struck her sharply in the chest, almost knocking her from the saddle, but that her need to make certain Matt and Uncle Sean were all right had been paramount.

She had thought it was her bullet that had killed Mason when she dismounted, but with several bullets lodged in his body when they examined him later, it could not be ascertained which one had been fatal.

Matt kissed her lightly and Samantha remembered the days that followed that confusion on the trail. Matt had insisted on certain formalities, and she had happily agreed to them. The result was that it wasn't merely Matt Strait whose arms now held her so close. It was her *husband*, Matt Strait.

The day of their wedding was a precious memory despite her weakness:

The sun had shone brightly and the air was warm as she walked unsteadily toward the altar of the small, nondenominational church in Winston where the part-time minister beamed as he awaited her. It had been difficult to walk, but she had insisted that she could. The effort had been almost as difficult as selecting the gown she wore—simple, white, trailing to the floor. But she had had Jenny to help her all the way because they had had a double wedding ceremony—suitable for twins who would remain close forever.

She remembered that Jenny and Randolph had walked down the aisle behind them while Uncle Sean walked in front with her, supporting her protectively, despite his wound, until the moment he gave her away. She recalled winking at a tearful Toby, who watched from the pews, and noted that Helen and Jim sat side by side holding hands. She recalled even more clearly that Matt awaited her at the altar beside his twin, but that Matt only had eyes for her.

Samantha's name was now Samantha Strait, and Jenny's was Jenny Conroy, the name Tucker had chosen to keep. She supposed that was fitting. As for the disposition of Tucker's criminal acts—

Samantha had learned later that Toby's disappearance on that fateful day was for a good cause. He had traveled to visit a fellow named Horace

Wells, whom both Jeremy Strait and he had known years earlier before Wells became a district judge. With Toby's petition for clemency, in addition to a written statement from celebrated Pinkerton Agent Sean McGill declaring Tucker's cooperation in apprehending the unfortunately now deceased Mason Light and Reggie Marks before turning himself in, Tucker had been given a short sentence.

The ending of that affair was suitable to all.

As for herself, Samantha realized it was too early to decide which direction her life would take from there. She was still recuperating and still uncertain if, as Samantha Strait, she would continue to pursue the career as a Pinkerton that had brought her to Winston. She was especially indecisive now that her focus had shifted so lovingly in another direction.

Samantha separated her lips under Matt's kiss. She sighed when Matt drew back and curved his arm around her.

Whatever she decided, she knew her father would be proud of her decision because her quest had brought her to the man she loved. And most importantly, because she was certain he would approve of Matt.

It occurred to her that her father would even approve of Tucker because he was paying the price for his crimes with a belated realization of the true meaning of love, and with the knowledge that Jenny was waiting.

Matt's whisper interrupted her thoughts. She turned toward him and indulged his loving gaze as his light eyes looked down into hers. She knew she would never tire of hearing him say the words "I love you."

Matt drew Samantha closer as her eyes drifted closed. He remembered his fear when he came so close to losing her. He had known at that moment he had been a fool to believe, however briefly, that he could let her go.

Matt kissed her lips lightly again, knowing he would never tire of the taste of her. He knew now that he had never been more right—and never more wrong—than when he first met Samantha. He had felt the instant attraction between them and he had known she was trouble. He was right. She *was* trouble. But he had not realized at the time that she would be worth every moment.

He also knew now that despite all the deceits practiced on both their parts, and all the conflicts between them, an ecstasy had emerged that would last a lifetime.

As for Tucker, his brother had made his peace with the past. Matt had already arranged that Tucker would have the inheritance their father would have left him if he had realized his other son was still alive. It would be waiting for him when he was released from prison. He had no doubt that a new life would begin for Tucker then.

Although Tucker would be the last to admit it, he and his brother had actually come to like each other. He suspected the change in Tucker was due mostly to Jenny, because Tucker realized how lucky he was to have her.

Matt brushed fragrant locks of hair from Samantha's forehead. She would soon be well and strong, and he knew that although Samantha was contrary and headstrong, no man was luckier than he to have a woman who had risked her life for him.

That thought stirred a familiar uneasiness inside Matt as Samantha's breathing became slow and even. He would make sure that she would never again be faced with a similar risk. Samantha didn't know it yet, but she would never endanger her life again as a Pinkerton agent—or sit on the lap of a possible bank robber with a sultry look in her eyes, just to solve a case. Her flirting days were now just for him.

As for that journey of loving years he envisioned Samantha and him taking, any journey of years began with a day.

Samantha whispered his name in her sleep, and Matt knew that day had already begun.

Epilogue

"When are you going to tell her?"

Sean faced Toby where they sat on a bench outside Toby's livery stable while sunshine bathed the main street of Winston. His brows drawing together in a frown, his wound still considered to be healing despite his objection that it was fine, Sean realized he had been reluctant to return to work anyway. With Samantha still on the mend, he preferred time off, which he had earned with Samantha's help by resolving a case that had stymied the Pinkerton Agency longer than most.

Sean recalled walking Samantha down the aisle. That had been a great moment for him—the realization of a dream he had cherished from the day of Tom Rigg's death. He knew he would never forget it.

Still, he responded darkly, "What do you mean?"

"I may be old, but I ain't blind," Toby responded with unexpected candor. "I saw the resemblance between you and Samantha when you first came to town."

Stunned, Sean replied, "There's no resemblance between Samantha and me."

"Maybe I have a sharper eye than most. I never saw you when you were her age, but I have a feeling that although your hair is white now, it was blond once. Maybe it wasn't as blond as Samantha's, maybe your skin is darkened by the sun and it ain't as fair as hers, but it's close enough." The old fellow added, "Yet it's your eyes that tell the tale."

"My eyes? They're not the same color as Samantha's."

"But I recognized the way you look at her. I looked at a baby that grew up to become a young woman the same way in another lifetime long ago. I was protective. I guided her. I would've done anything for her, but she was determined to go her own way. It didn't work out for me and I don't talk about it no more, but I recognized that same light in your eyes when you looked at Samantha. It's that combination of love and concern, and a determination not to interfere with her mature choices—but just to be there in case she needs you."

Sean remained silent.

"I got a second chance with Samantha, but I'm not so sure you'll be as lucky as me. You should tell her."

"Tell her what?" Sean responded unexpectedly.

"Do you think I'm proud of the fact that I panicked when the woman who gave birth to her—the woman I had loved but never married—died in childbirth; that I gave her over to my best friend who was married to a wonderful but barren woman to raise in my stead? Or maybe that I saw Samantha react the same way to Matt's name as I reacted when Marian's name was mentioned, and that I knew instinctively what it meant?"

Sean shook his head without waiting for a reply. "No, I don't think I'll tell her."

He continued tightly. "Samantha idolized Tom Rigg. Margaret Rigg died unexpectedly when Samantha was young. I had my chance then, but I couldn't take it. Samantha clung to Tom even more steadfastly and I couldn't take the only stability she had known away from her."

"So that's how you became Uncle Sean."

"I was Uncle Sean long before that."

"Still—"

"I was proud of her in every way, Toby. She was strong, resourceful, determined, and she loved me—I knew she did. She turned to me every time she felt overwhelmed after Tom died, and I was always there for her, just like now. I was pleased with the way Tom had raised her and proud of the woman she had become. I knew I could never have done a better job than he did."

"Tom's gone now."

"But Samantha's memories of him and the sense of self he instilled in her aren't. I won't take that away from her with selfish motives."

"You do realize that no children will ever call you Grandpa?"

"Maybe not. Maybe I'll never get to hear Samantha call me by the name I rightly deserve, but I intend sticking around just long enough to play whatever part she wants me to play in her life."

Sean's blue eyes narrowed with concerned assessment when he looked at the older man. "My question now is what you intend to do."

Momentarily silent, Toby then responded, "I'll do the same as you, I guess." Sean was unable to reply when Toby continued thoughtfully. "I don't think it would be too smart to do anything else when you've obviously thought a lot about it all."

"Thanks." Sean extended his hand.

Toby shook it hard, adding, "Just promise that you'll let me know if you change your mind about telling Samantha that she's really your daughter."

Toby's words took a visible toll on Sean as he replied, "I promise." He took a moment and then continued. "I guess it's good for someone besides me to know the truth. I lost a good friend when I lost Tom, but because of Samantha, I found another."

Sean continued softly. "It's only fitting somehow that my new good friend should share the secret that another good friend of mine did. I don't think I can expect more."

278

Sean did not pause to see Toby's eyes fill expressively. Instead, he stood up and sauntered away with a tip of his hat and a deceptively casual tread.

A year later, Sean's expression glowed when Samantha walked across the Double S yard to greet him with Matt beside her. She held her new son out to him as she said to the gurgling baby, "Look, Matthew Thomas, Grandpa Sean is waiting to hold you."

Sean supposed he would never know if Samantha had discovered his secret, but it didn't matter. He knew he would never be more proud than he was at that moment when he held his grandson in his arms.

Amidst the laughter and the smiles, well and strong at last, Samantha looked up at Matt. She had decided to put off any Pinkerton involvement for the time being. After all, she was happy and content. Matt was her baby's father and both their baby and he loved her.

Could she ask for more?

Author's Note

One of my favorite memories is the trip my husband and I took to San Antonio, Texas, where we visited with author friends. Among them were Constance O'Banyon and her husband, Jim.

I ordered biscuits at every meal when we ate out. Constance and her husband appeared surprised that I was so taken with them. I explained that there was something special about the biscuits in Texas.

Before I left, Constance handed me a biscuit cutter and her aunt Ethyl's biscuit recipe, which her family has been using for years.

I've treasured this recipe. I hope you enjoy it as well.

Constance also supplied the recipe for Golden Texas Corn Bread (also a genuine Texas recipe) that follows.

Thank you, Constance O'Banyon.

Aunt Ethyl's Biscuits

5 c. flour
½ c. sugar
½ c. shortening
4 tsp. baking powder
½ tsp. baking soda
1 tsp. salt
2 c. buttermilk
2 packages yeast

Mix dry ingredients. Put dissolved yeast in buttermilk and add to mix. Knead. Shape into biscuits and let rise 15 minutes (or a few minutes longer if necessary).

Bake at 375 degrees about 15 minutes. (Biscuits will continue to rise while baking.)

Note:

Unused dough can be stored in refrigerator.

Please note that genuine buttermilk is a necessary ingredient for this and the following recipe. No substitutes should be added.

Golden Texas Corn Bread

1 c. cornmeal (white or yellow)
1 c. flour
¼ c. sugar
4 tsp. baking powder
½ tsp. salt
1 egg
1 c. buttermilk

Mix and put in greased *iron skillet*. Bake at 425 degrees for 20 to 25 minutes. (If mixture is too dry, add a little buttermilk.)

Note:

An iron skillet is needed for authentic Texas cooking.

A trick to obtain a golden crust on your corn bread is to grease the skillet and to put it on the stove for a few minutes until the bottom has browned. It has to be watched carefully so it won't burn. Then put the skillet in the oven and bake as indicated.

Enjoy!

Discover Great Native American Romance

BLACK HORSE
Veronica Blake
Read on for a sneak preview.

"See? That's him, that's Black Horse," Gentle Water whispered. She put her hand over her mouth and stifled a giggle.

"Quiet! He might hear us," Meadow warned with a stern glance. She tried to look serious, but the sight of the young war chief on the other side of the thick brush sent her heartbeat racing and caused a strange fluttering sensation in the pit of her stomach. She turned away from Gentle Water and focused on the man down by the riverbank.

Even from this distance he appeared to be slightly taller than most of the Sioux men in their village. Two thin braids wound with brass wires framed his handsome face and dangled over his bare chest. The rest of his dark hair hung to his waist. A large necklace of grizzly-bear claws encircled his neck—potent medicine for a warrior to possess. Black Horse was a chief warrior, which at his young age meant that he held a powerful position in the tribe.

Everything about him was impressive, Meadow noticed. His shoulders were outlined with bulging, sinewy muscles, his belly lean and defined. A white breechcloth encircled his hips, and tan leather leggings hugged his muscular thighs.

"Do you want to meet him now?" Gentle Water asked. Her voice rose slightly above a whisper. She muffled another giggle when her friend shook her fist at her. Gentle

Water leaned close to the other girl. "Your face is red, Meadow. I think you want to do more than just meet him."

"I'm leaving," Meadow whispered through gritted teeth. Before she could turn around to crawl back through the thick brush, a deep voice bellowed from the riverbank below.

"Who's there?"

Meadow instinctively fell down flat on her stomach and held her breath. Pressed against the hard ground, she could feel her heartbeat thudding uncontrollably. Beside her, Gentle Water was also lying facedown in the underbrush. But now she was also being quiet as death. Meadow silently cursed herself for letting Gentle Water talk her into coming down to the river today. Nothing could be more humiliating than getting caught in this compromising position.

When his cry was met with silence, Black Horse grew wary. He pulled his antler-handled knife from the sheath at his hip, bent his knees and began to inch up the sloping riverbank. His dark eyes darted back and forth. The dense brush of alders and willows made it difficult for him to see. Black Horse knew how easy it was to hide in heavy brush such as this. He had done so on many occasions when he had been hunting game, or waiting in ambush for an enemy.

Sensing there was someone—or something—hiding in the bushes, Black Horse didn't call out again. He continued to take cautious steps toward the bushes. He had moved only a few feet, though, when his keen ears picked up the slight sound of rustling brush. His footsteps halted. Every muscle in his body tensed. A light sheen of perspiration broke out on his chest and face as he prepared to go to battle again.

For several moments Black Horse did not move. When another faint sound came from the bushes, he pinpointed his prey's location. He moved like a crouched mountain lion toward the bushes to his left and then peered into the heavy underbrush. He smiled.

Through the low-hanging branches of the willows he could see the distinct forms of two females lying face-down on the ground. He studied them for a moment. Black Horse was certain they were just a couple of curious young girls. His smile widened.

"I must have been imagining things," he said out loud. The girls did not move a muscle. The urge to chuckle tickled the back of his throat, but he resisted.

As he sheathed his knife, he turned and walked back to the river with a nonchalant stride. Humming to himself, Black Horse untied the belt that held his elaborately decorated knife sheath. He placed the weapon down on the ground, then presented his observers with a full view of his hind side as he bent over to pull off his tall, beaded moccasins. He kept his movements slow and provocative. I'll give them something to see, he thought.

Unable to keep the smirk from his lips, Black Horse kept his back to the bushes until he could control his expression. He wanted to make sure that the girls were still watching. He didn't want to waste all this effort if he no longer had an audience. With a feigned look of indifference, he turned around. There were still no signs of movement on the hillside.

Black Horse untied the belt that held up his leggings. He rolled the fringed leg coverings down past his knees, lifted one foot up, then the other, until he was free of the leggings. Clothed only in his breechcloth, he turned toward the river again. He remained in this position for a moment to give the two visitors a chance to leave before they saw more than they were expecting. Or maybe that's what they want, he told himself. Why else would they be hiding in the bushes while he was preparing to take a bath? He turned sideways to the bushes where his audience hid, and slowly untied the strings at his hip.

In the scanty cover of the bushes, Meadow watched every one of Black Horse's movements in breathless awe. He was the most magnificent man she had ever seen, and the way he was undressing was like nothing she had ever witnessed. In the pit of her stomach, and even lower, she felt an unfamiliar ache. Her insides were on fire, and every time Black Horse discarded another article of clothing, the heat within her grew more consuming.

He was facing the bushes now, and Meadow knew there was no way they could leave without being seen. They would have to wait until he was in the water. Then, they could flee. Once they were away from the river, she planned to tell Gentle Water what a troublemaker she was to have suggested this scheme. But now that they were here she could not tear her gaze from the warrior's seductive movements.

His stark white breechcloth made the young chief's smooth skin shine like glistening copper. His legs were long, with well-defined muscles along his thighs and on the backs of his calves. As he moved, every muscle of his body strained and contracted with exact precision. At that moment, Meadow could not have taken her eyes off him even if the bushes around her had caught on fire and burned to the ground.

When the ties that held his breechcloth together were dangling long and loose in his hands, Black Horse was still facing the bushes. He parted his powerful thighs as he slowly pulled the breechcloth out from between his legs and then casually let it drop on the ground at his feet.

Meadow felt perspiration running down her body as she continued to stare. She had seen very young boys running around naked in the village, and she'd helped her adoptive mother prepare dead men for burial. She knew what a male looked like without his breechcloth. But little boys and dead men did not even begin to compare to the virile male who stood at the river's edge now.

Yearnings that Meadow had never experienced before ballooned inside her until she thought she would burst apart. It seemed as if Black Horse knew he had an audience. But that was ridiculous; he had no idea they were hiding here in the bushes. As soon as he dove into the water, they would get away from here, and this embarrassing situation could be forgotten. Even as that thought passed through her mind, Meadow knew there was no way that she would ever be able to forget the sight of this handsome man, who now stood before her naked as a newborn babe.

The gasps coming from the thick brush almost made Black Horse laugh out loud. More than anything, he wished he could see the faces of his inquisitive observers. He knew, however, it would not be long before he would encounter at least one of them again. When he saw them hiding in the underbrush, he had noticed one of them had hair that was the shade of the prairie sun—a half-breed, most likely. She would be easy to find in the Sioux village, where most of the woman had hair as black as midnight.

Smug and filled with satisfaction that he'd given the curious virgins an eyeful, Black Horse lingered for a second longer. As though he had grown bored with the charade, he turned and sauntered to the river's edge. Without pausing, he walked into the cool water until it was up to his hips and then dove under the surface.

Staying completely submerged, he swam out to the middle before coming up for air. He turned back toward the bushes.

A deep laugh escaped Black Horse when he glimpsed the two spies hurrying up the hillside on the other side of the thick clump of bushes. They were both dressed in the long fringed dresses and knee-high moccasins worn by all the females of the tribe, but the thing that caught his attention the most was the alluring way the buckskin dress caressed the curvy hips of the taller one—the one with the long yellow hair.

Black Horse began to splash around in the deep water of the river. He let the cool water wash away the dirt from the last of the long, hard trails he had ridden for the past few months. For a while, he let his mind clear. At dawn this morning he had crossed the Canadian border. He hoped Canada would offer a peaceful haven where he could rest.

Barely more than three months ago he had ridden with his comrades in the battle at Greasy Grass River—the battleground the white men called Little Bighorn. But victory over the long-haired General Custer and his men had been short-lived. Within weeks of that successful attack, Black Horse's people had been defeated again and again.

But for the first time in a long time he had something besides fighting and killing on his mind. He was thinking of the two girls in the bushes, and of the fun he would have when he had a chance to meet the light haired one face-to-face. His mind recalled the way the wavy locks of her flaxen hair had swung back and forth above her shapely hips as she scurried up the hillside. He hoped she looked as enticing from the front as she did from behind. Another carefree laugh escaped from his mouth. He was looking forward to his stay here in Canada.

INTERACT WITH DORCHESTER ONLINE!

Want to learn more about your favorite books and authors?
Want to talk with other readers that like to read the same books as you?
Want to see up-to-the-minute Dorchester news?

VISIT DORCHESTER AT:
DorchesterPub.com
Twitter.com/DorchesterPub
Facebook.com (Search Pages)

DISCUSS DORCHESTER'S NOVELS AT:
Dorchester Forums at DorchesterPub.com
GoodReads.com
LibraryThing.com
Myspace.com/books
Shelfari.com
WeRead.com

Dawn McTavish

A HARD MAN

Trace Ord was a renegade rider, a wrangler sent to round up horses that strayed or were rustled from their owners. He was born to the saddle and could shoot the wings off a bee in flight, and he'd seen his share of action. A man like himself couldn't live past thirty in post–Civil War Arizona and not come up against some bandit or cardsharp itching to throw lead.

A HARDER SITUATION

His current job had Trace working for two ranchers up north who were certain he'd find their stock at the Lazy C. Getting those horses back would be anything but easy. The owner of the Lazy C was as mean as any hombre living, and he and his men were more than willing to trade bullets. His wife was a touch more dangerous. The desperate beauty found Trace on the plains . . . and she stole both his prize stallion and his heart.

Renegade Riders

ISBN 13: 978-0-8439-6322-9

The Randolph brothers were a wild bunch—carving an empire out of the rugged land, fighting off rustlers and Mexican bandits—and they weren't about to let any female change their ways . . . not until a woman's touch turned their lives upside down and made them lose their hearts.

The Seven Brides series

Rose
Fern
Iris
Laurel
(Coming next year)
Lily
Violet
Daisy

"Leigh Greenwood's memorable characters work their way into your heart. I'm sure you will come to love them as much as Rose, Fern, George and the rest of the unforgettable Randolph clan." —Kathe Robin, *RT Book Reviews*

CONSTANCE O'BANYON

"Ms. O'Banyon is an author that knows how to hook a reader and keep them riveted."
—Fresh Fiction

Wolf Runner

He Would Teach Her

All Cheyenne ever wanted was to know where she belonged. Daughter of a white man and a native woman, she lived as an outcast among the white people of New Mexico and never knew anyone that was like her. Until the day he stepped off the train. Wolf Runner was his name and he, too, was a half-breed. She was drawn to him, to the kindred spirit she felt within him. He would reveal to her the mysteries of his Blackfoot people. He would show her how to walk tall in the presence of the white man. He would let her run wild with him in his Rocky Mountains alongside the wolves. And beneath the silvery light of a Montana moon, his seduction would awaken her maiden's heart and . . .

He Would Love Her

ISBN 13: 978-0-8439-6439-4

☐ **YES!**

Sign me up for the Historical Romance Book Club and send my FREE BOOKS! If I choose to stay in the club, I will pay only $8.50* each month, a savings of $6.48!

NAME: _____

ADDRESS: _____

TELEPHONE: _____

EMAIL: _____

☐ I want to pay by credit card.

☐ **VISA**　☐ **MasterCard.**　☐ **DISCOVER**

ACCOUNT #: _____

EXPIRATION DATE: _____

SIGNATURE: _____

Mail this page along with $2.00 shipping and handling to:
Historical Romance Book Club
PO Box 6640
Wayne, PA 19087
Or fax (must include credit card information) to:
610-995-9274
You can also sign up online at **www.dorchesterpub.com**.
*Plus $2.00 for shipping. Offer open to residents of the U.S. and Canada only.
Canadian residents please call 1-800-481-9191 for pricing information.
If under 18, a parent or guardian must sign. Terms, prices and conditions subject to change. Subscription subject to acceptance. Dorchester Publishing reserves the right to reject any order or cancel any subscription.